When All the World's Asleep

Manuel Magaña

ISBN 979-8-9916517-0-7 (sc)
ISBN 979-8-9916517-1-4 (hc)

ACKNOWLEDGEMENTS:

To my wife, Rosa Magaña. Thank you for all your love, patience, and encouragement throughout our life and this writing process. I could not have done it without you. You make me a better man.

Thank you, Eduardo Fisher, my lifetime friend, for your great editorial feedback. Your fresh eyes helped me cross the finish line.

Thank you, Randy Ingermanson, my friend and former fiction-writing instructor, for your great insights and encouraging spirit.

And thank you, Gregory Mitchell, for allowing me to use your photo of the Rio Vista Bridge as my book cover. You bring the Sacramento River Delta to life.

WHEN ALL THE WORLD'S ASLEEP

Antonio Quintero knocked again on the locked, glass doors of Rio Vista High School. When a brunette stepped out of the main office, the sight of her dug a stake in his heart. He expected her to have gone home by now. His innards churned. He even considered walking away.

But it was too late.

She opened the door.

"Stacey?" said Antonio.

The soft pronunciation seemed to catch her off guard. She scrutinized his beard. "Antonio! Oh, my God." She threw open the door and wrapped her arms around him.

He froze for a moment, then responded with a polite tap on the back.

"What on earth are you doing here?" she said.

"Oh . . . just a little forced vacation."

She released him with a frown, waiting to hear more, but Antonio remained silent.

"Forced?"

"I'll have to tell you later. I was hoping to see John."

"He didn't tell me you were coming."

"He doesn't know."

Her face expressed genuine concern. "Please don't treat me like a stranger. I'm still in your corner, you know. In spite of everything."

Antonio blinked. "I just needed to get away for a while. It's a long story."

Her wary eyes looked him over. "Are you gonna be around for a while?"

"Not sure. What are *you* still doing here?"

"Just catching up on some work. I—" She stopped herself. "I'll walk you over to John's classroom."

He grabbed his duffel bag. They walked to the end of the hallway, turned right, and stopped at the second door to their left.

"Let me surprise him."

She motioned for Antonio to hold back and opened the door. She stuck her head in.

"John, you have a visitor."

John Keefe looked up from his student's essays. "Visitor? At his hour? I don't think I have the energy."

She walked in with Antonio behind her. "Not even for your favorite alumnus?"

"Antonio!" John dropped everything. "What the heck are you doing here?"

Antonio grinned. "It's good to see you, too."

John stood up his plump, five-foot-six frame, looking confused. Antonio rounded the desk. They shook hands and embraced with purpose.

"Why didn't you tell me you were coming?" said John.

"I wanted to make sure I made it first."

"Everything okay?"

"Not quite."

John eyeballed him. "Spit it out."

Stacey gazed at John, then Antonio, and took the hint. "I'll let you guys talk."

Antonio turned. "I'll see you later, Stacey."

She smiled and walked back to her office.

. . . .

"She's been thinking about you," said John.

Antonio scoffed, "Come on, John."

"I'm just saying." John raised his shoulders and tilted his head innocuously. "Anyway, how are the brothers treating you? Have they finally had enough of your antics?"

Antonio took a seat in front of John's desk without saying a word.

John kept his eyes on him.

"I don't think I can go back to Mexico for a while," said Antonio.

John scowled. "What the heck happened?"

"Well, you know how things started getting complicated when I moved to Zamora."

"I told you to be careful."

"I know, but I couldn't sit around and do nothing?"

An awkward silence ensued. They gazed up and down at each other.

"How can I help?" said John.

"You think I can stay with you for a while, at least until I straighten out a few things?"

"As long as you want. You know that."

Antonio acknowledged with a nod, then glanced out the wall of windows to his left, grappling with reminiscences of Stacey. "How's my brother Gary?"

"He says he loves D.C. I can't imagine why."

"His new job's going well, I assume."

"Oh yeah! It's only a research job, but he says he's making good contacts."

Antonio leaned back in his chair.

"Have you spoken to your brother Rubén?" said John.

"I spent a couple days with him before coming here."

"Does he know what's going on?"

"I told him."

"What'd he say?"

"He wanted me to stay with him for a while, but I told him I needed to see you."

"Did you ask him when he's gonna come and visit? He hasn't called in about a month."

Antonio grinned. "He hasn't forgotten you, John. They just have him running up and down the state at the moment. I was lucky to see him myself."

"I can imagine." He shoved some papers in a folder. "How 'bout going out for a drink?"

"What about your work?"

John threw his hands up in the air. "I've been here too long as it is."

"Rubén tells me you still spend your evenings here."

"Ah, don't listen to stories." John gave a sly smile. "You wanna invite Stacey?"

"That's probably not a good idea."

"Why not?" John put on an air of innocence. "Put a little adventure into your life."

Antonio's brows narrowed. "I think I've had a little too much lately."

"Come on. I won't be inappropriate."

Antonio tried to remain serious, but he had to chuckle. "Fine, but you really need to behave."

"Great! Let's go get her."

John put on his jacket and grabbed his things.

When they reached the office, John knocked on the door and stuck his head in without waiting for a response.

Eighties music funneled out of the radio on Stacey's desk.

"I was wondering if you'd like to join us for a drink," said John.

Stacey reached across her desk to turn off the radio.

"Right now?"

"Why not?"

She gave John a blank look. "Give me a few minutes. I have to finish something. What if I meet you guys there?"

"Sounds great."

"Where you going?"

"Foster's Bighorn."

"Okay. See you there."

John winked at Antonio as they walked out. "I'm telling you."

"She's still married, for God's sake." Antonio pushed the front door open with his bag.

"She's getting divorced."

"And?" said Antonio. "What does that have to do with anything?"

John smiled. "There's nothing wrong with testing the strength of your calling, is there?"

"What're you talking about?"

John stopped and faced Antonio. "Look, I know what the priesthood means to you, and I'm not trying to belittle it, but I know there's another force at work here—at least as strong, if not stronger. Let's face it, you hesitated in coming to see me, didn't you? You were afraid of what might happen if you saw her."

"John, please."

"What's the harm? You're not a priest yet. Maybe there's still hope."

"That's not why I came."

"Look at *me*," said John. "I haven't even dated since Beth passed away, and let me tell you, it's no good for a man to be alone. There's still time to reevaluate your service to God. I don't think He'd mind that much. Really. I'm sure He'd like to see both of you happy."

"I don't wanna talk about this right now."

"Why not?"

"I've got a lot on my mind."

"That's fine, but I'm telling you, circumstances won't get any better."

CHAPTER 2

Antonio ruminated as John steered his way through the fog-filled streets. No matter how familiar the drive, caution ruled under such conditions. John had turned on the heater, but before it could have much effect, they pulled into a spot on Main Street and scurried up to the balmy entrance of Foster's Bighorn.

"Ha ya doin', Mr. Keefe?" said a young man, smoking a cigarette at the bar.

"Great, Brian." John shook off the lingering nip. "What's new with you?"

"I got the job at Amerada Hess."

"Excellent! Glad to hear it."

"Thanks for the good word."

John nodded. "Any time."

They sat at a table between the bar and the dining area. Business was slow for a Friday evening. Only about a quarter full. The place felt cozy, yet big enough to display one of the largest collections of wild game trophies in the world. The original owner, William Foster, had been an avid hunter in the African plains—as the pictures lining the back wall proclaimed. He posed over various kills, prominently displaying his rifle in hand. Behind John hung the elephant head, with its trunk reaching out into the dim, murky air. The rhinoceros and buffalo, among other game, adorned the opposite wall. Yet John's and Antonio's favorite piece remained the silly jackrabbit propped up next to the cash register at the bar.

Antonio asked for two beers.

John sat across the table, with the faint light emphasizing the gray of his beard. Had it not been well-trimmed, it would have made him look older than his mid-fifties.

"So," said Antonio, "tell me more about that lady you wrote me about."

"What lady?"

"The one you were impressed with."

"I said no such thing. All I said is that her son reminded me of you."

"True," said Antonio with a smile. "Yet you know exactly who I'm talking about."

John took a swig of his beer. "Her son's in my sophomore English class this year." And he quickly dismissed the matter, "She's a widow."

"I see!" Antonio grinned. "Should I be calling you Zorba the Greek now?" He paused for effect. "The widow seeker."

"Cut it out."

"I'm sorry." Antonio almost chuckled. "Please continue."

"I can't afford a conflict-of-interest with her son. Besides, she's Mexican and probably not interested in going out with a half-gringo."

"How would you know?"

John shrugged.

"How'd you meet her?"

"The grocery store. She was with her son."

"Interesting choice of venue."

"It wasn't a choice."

"Fate?"

"I don't think so! Besides, she's too young for me. And my Spanish isn't what it used to be." He pointed his beer at Antonio. "At least I can practice more—now that you're back."

"Now that I'm back?" Antonio transitioned to Spanish. "What would your mom say about this?"

"I know, I know," said John, practicing his Spanish. "She would also be devastated that I hardly remember the taste of her *buñuelos*."

"No kidding! But don't change the subject. When are you gonna call this lady?"

"I'm not calling *anybody*."

"Really?" Antonio saw his opportunity. "Then don't get pushy about Stacey. Besides, there's nothing wrong with your Spanish."

"It's not the same thing, Antonio. You can't compare me with you. I lived a good life already. You and Stacey have both been through a lot. It hurts me to see the two of you unhappy."

"Having lived a good life doesn't give you license to throw the rest of it away."

"True, but I'm not throwing anything away. I have plenty to live for."

"Then why not make it even better by giving this lady a call?"

"I told you, I'd rather not. I'm not sure how her son would take it."

"Does he like you?"

"I suppose."

"Is he a good student?"

"Yes—very good."

"Then you have nothing to worry about."

"Of course, I do. The more I care about someone, the harder I push them. You know that."

"Oh, yeah!" Antonio reflected. "That was quite frustrating. Not to mention unfair. What about extra tutoring? I bet his mom would love that."

"I can't. It wouldn't be fair to the other students."

"Dang!" Antonio reverted to English. "You're as difficult as ever."

"*Me?*" said John, also in English. "If I am, it's only because I had to deal with strong-willed kids like you."

Antonio took a deep breath. "How 'bout getting back to our Spanish lesson?"

"*Por supuesto.*"

The front doors opened, and three soldiers dressed in camo walked in. They took a seat at the bar and ordered a round of beer.

John recognized the one on the left.

"That's Mike Lacey," said John, still in Spanish.

"A relative of Don's?" said Antonio.

"His nephew."

"I wonder if he has his temperament." He reached for his ankle. "That break still hurts every once in a while."

"It was a nasty break."

"At least you kicked Don off the team."

"It was the least he deserved."

"No kidding. I can't believe how competitive he was." Antonio's face struggled with his next thought. "And he didn't stop until he took what was most important to me."

John fired back. "That only happened because you left for the Army."

"I don't know if that was the only reason—" he stopped himself. "But she never did understand."

John nodded.

"Heck! We might even be married, and I wouldn't be in this predicament."

John restrained himself. "Are you gonna tell me what happened, or what?"

"I'll tell you later."

"Tell me now."

"Later, John. I need some time." He raised his beer. "Let's just drink to life—even to Don." He motioned with his head "And Mike over there."

Mike looked over, not liking the fact that he had heard his name in conversation.

"Jack tells me Don hasn't gotten any better," Antonio continued in Spanish.

Mike's eyes narrowed, and a scowl crossed his face.

"Not much," said John. "He thinks he runs the town ever since he became police chief."

"Yeah, that's what I heard. How'd he get appointed anyway?"

"I guess he kissed a lot of babies—and a few other things."

Laughter returned to the conversation.

"Hey," said Mike, "why don't you speak some English over there?"

"Relax," said John. "We're just catching up."

John rolled his eyes at Antonio.

"Then show some respect," said Mike. "We speak English around here."

John and Antonio held their tongue.

"Did you hear what I said?"

"We heard you," said Antonio.

"You better!"

Antonio tempered his tone. "You know, it's quite an honor to wear that uniform."

"What the hell would you know?"

"Enough to know that we need to be willing to die for others."

"Just mind your own damn business," said Mike. "And speak some English."

Antonio turned back to John.

"Did you hear what I said?"

Antonio did not respond.

"Did you hear what I said?"

"I heard you," said Antonio, keeping his eyes on John. "Why don't you enjoy your beer with your friends? We're just trying to do the same."

Mike swiveled in their direction. "Who the hell do you think you are—giving out orders?"

"I'm just a friend of John's."

"Well, I don't like hearin' my name in other people's conversations."

Antonio acknowledged. "Fair enough."

"Then why don't you keep my uncle's name out of it too? He's the police chief, you know."

"That's what we were discussing," said John.

Mike kept his eyes on Antonio. "Then show some respect."

Antonio turned away.

"Did you hear what I said?"

"Come on, Mike," said the bartender.

Antonio remained silent.

"Are you hard of hearin', or what? I asked you a question."

Antonio's body stiffened. "Look, kid, you're not the only one who knows what it is to wear that uniform, so please don't come around demanding respect when you don't even know what's going on. Just relax and enjoy the time with your friends. Nobody's looking for trouble."

Mike jumped off his stool.

"Hey, guys," he called to his friends, "why don't you come over and say hi?"

Brian turned from the other end of the bar. "Just cool it," he said. "He ain't doin' nothin' to you guys."

"Why don't *you* mind your own business?" said Mike, the veins in his temples beginning to bulge.

"Just forget it, Mike," said one of the soldiers.

"Come on, guys. Don't wuss out on me."

"What are you trying to do?" said John.

"Butt out, Mr. Keefe. This friend of yours needs to learn what it is to have respect."

John jumped to his feet. "Mike, just relax. Go and have a seat with your friends."

"Don't tell me what to do, Mr. Keefe."

John moved in between Mike and Antonio.

Mike's eyes went wild. He lunged forward and shoved John to the side.

John staggered, slammed into a chair and onto the floor.

Mike stepped right over him, toward Antonio.

Antonio scrambled toward John.

Mike tried to shove him, but Antonio grabbed his arm, yanked him to the side, twisted him around, and slammed him face-first onto the floor with his arm locked behind his back.

All eyes in the room turned to stare.

"Why don't you stop this crap before someone gets hurt?" said Antonio.

He released Mike and went to look after John. "Are you okay?"

"I'm all right," said John, trying to sit up. "That little shit."

One of Mike's buddies came up behind him. "Take it easy, man."

Mike shrugged him off as he got to his feet.

Antonio tried to ignore him, but out of the corner of his eye, he saw Mike reach for a chair and circle around to his blind side.

"Watch out!" said Brian.

Antonio heaved John to the side, but not before the chair smashed John's left arm with a hollow thunk.

John bellowed miserably.

Antonio thrust himself up—shoulders high—and confronted Mike. "You son-of-a—."

"What's the matter? You forgot what it's like to be in combat?"

"Have you even found out what it's like?"

Mike lost his composure, then squatted into an offensive stance.

Repulsed, Antonio returned his attention to John. "You okay?"

Behind him, once again, came the clear sound of motion. The creaking sound of another chair being swung hard.

Antonio threw his body into a full-turn kick that connected with Mike's face.

Mike flew across the table behind him and onto the floor. He grabbed his bloody face. "You son-of-a-bitch. You broke my nose." He turned to the bartender. "Call the police, Doug. See what this bastard does now."

"Just back off!" said Antonio.

"You okay, Mike?" his friends asked.

"I'm fine! Just make sure this bastard doesn't run outta here."

Antonio helped John to his feet.

"I'm okay," he said, holding his arm.

"You sure it's not broken?"

"No—" He winced, pulling his arm up close to his body. "—but it's gonna be awfully sore for a while."

"Damn kid," said Antonio.

"Don't worry," said John. "He asked for it."

"I didn't ask for shit. It's your damn friend that started talking crap." Mike held a bundle of napkins to his nose.

The entire place had gone quiet with everyone staring.

"What the hell you all lookin' at?" said Mike.

The front door swung open, and Stacey walked in. She immediately noticed that Mike and John were hurt. "What's going on?" she demanded.

No one answered.

She cautiously walked over to John. "What happened?"

"This damn nephew of yours almost broke my arm. Antonio tried to help me."

Stacey turned around. "What happened, Mike?"

"You gonna believe this shit? It's that son-of-a-bitch's fault."

"Come on, Mike. I know you."

"Shit! You gonna turn on me, too?"

"That's not what this is about, Mike."

She walked over to him and tried to look at his nose.

He yanked himself away.

"Let me take you to the doctor."

"I don't need your damn help. Don's comin' over right now. He'll take care o' this."

"Fine!" she said. "We'll wait."

She walked to the bar and asked for a double margarita on the rocks. After taking a swig, she went to sit with John and Antonio.

"Sorry I'm late," she said. "Maybe I could've helped."

"Don't worry," said John. "It's over."

. . . .

Don Lacey walked into Foster's with his baton in hand and Officer Albert McCabe behind him. Don's balding, red hair and tight face properly complemented his caustic, penetrating stare—the stare he worked so long to perfect. He walked with his head up high and a soldierly stride; and even though his uniform gripped an extra ten pounds at the waist, he did not seem to mind or notice.

"Don!" said Mike.

"What happened here?"

"This son-of-a-bitch broke my nose."

"Mike started the whole thing," John protested.

When Don saw Stacey sitting with him and Antonio, his frame stiffened all the more. "We'll see about that." He strutted over to Stacey. "Why don't you go home?"

"Go to hell, Don. I don't have to go anywhere."

He clenched his jaw, and his face turned slightly red. He stared at her for a moment before turning to Antonio. "Qüin-tero, right?"

"That's right. If you insist on mispronouncing it."

"Get up and spread 'em."

"What for?"

"*What* are you doing?" said Stacey.

Don pointed his baton at her. "You stay out of this."

"I told you Mike started the whole damn thing," said John.

"That's right," said Brian.

Don turned abruptly. "When I ask you something, *then* you can speak."

Brian looked away in frustration.

"Qüintero, *you* get up!" said Don. "You have the right to remain silent."

Mike cackled. "Whattaya say now, huh?"

"Shut the hell up!" said Don.

He continued to read Antonio his Miranda rights.

"What about John's arm?" said Antonio. "What're you gonna do about that?"

"Is it broken?" Don asked.

"No, but barely."

"What the hell does that matter?" said Stacey.

"Then I guess there's nothin' to do," said Don.

"Bullcrap!" said John. "I want you to arrest this bastard nephew of yours for assault and battery."

Don examined him with penetrating eyes. "Are you pressin' charges?"

"If that's what it takes."

Don thought for a moment, then turned to Mike.

"Come on, Don. You can't do that to me."

Don continued to glare in his direction. "This could get messy."

"Damn, piece of shit." Mike stood motionless. "What if we just let 'm go?"

"Just get the hell out of here then," said John.

Don tightened the grip on his baton. He glowered at John, then leaned over and whispering into Antonio's ear, "You better watch yourself, Qüin-tero."

"I'd've thought you got over things by now," Antonio whispered back.

Don's nostrils dilated. "Don't push me." He took a long breath and let it out slowly, before turning to Mike in a normal tone of voice, "Let's get you to a doctor. It looks pretty bad." He went up to him and examined his nose. Then he raised his voice for everyone to hear. "Let's go. We'll ask the judge to issue a restraining order tomorrow."

Mike gave Antonio one last sneer as he walked out with Don.

CHAPTER 3

Mike and his friends stepped outside, burrowing their hands in their pockets. Everyone, except for Don who was hardly breathing, let out a heavy cloud of breath.

Mike tilted his head upward, exposing his nose to the lingering haze. The fog's numbing effect soothed him just right. "I can't believe this shit."

"Shut the hell up," said Don. He threw open the passenger door of his patrol vehicle, which was double-parked. "Get in. Albert'll take your friends home."

"Why? They're with me."

"Not right now they ain't."

Mike frowned painfully and turned to his friends. "I'll see you guys in a while."

"Sure, Mike," said one of the soldiers.

Mike slid into the car, and Don slammed the door behind him. He walked around to the driver's side and sat behind the wheel, glaring at Mike.

"What?" said Mike.

Don kept staring. "Don't *ever* pull this shit again."

"I told you—it wasn't my fault."

Don jerked the car into gear and skidded down Main Street.

"Take it easy, Don. This shit hurts."

"I don't give a *damn* if it was your fault or not. Next time, make sure there's no damn witnesses. You have to be *smart*." He tapped his own forehead with the tip of his fingers. "You have to do things *right*. Otherwise, don't get me involved."

"What's the big deal?"

"*What's the big deal?* It took me years to get to where I am. I'm not gonna let some stupid shit come along and make me look like an idiot. Everyone in this town respects me, you understand?"

Mike nodded slightly, still holding the napkins to his nose.

"If you *ever* make me look bad again, I swear I'll bust your nose myself."

Mike sighed, retreating into himself.

. . . .

Don kept his gaze straight ahead, consumed with the image of Stacey sitting with Antonio. He turned left onto Second Street and continued into the blinding fog of the Sacramento River.

Not once did he glance over at Mike.

As old memories of Stacey flashed before him, he questioned whether their years together meant anything to her at all. It burned him inside. He couldn't understand why the hell she left. As far as he was concerned, things weren't so bad, and if she'd been more patient, everything would've worked out fine. He was sure of it.

He hated losing control of a situation!

And never in his life did he expect Qüintero back in the picture. Don remembered him being a priest, or something. Unless it was all a sham. Whatever the case, he'd be damned if he let Qüintero take Stacey back. She belonged to him, not some damn old fling.

Don slowed down as he drove into the Sandy Beach parking lot, about a mile and a half out of town.

He couldn't think of a better place for Mike.

It used to be nothing but a gravel clearing. Don's father had brought him there once—to teach him a lesson—after getting caught for shoplifting. He threatened to drown him for what he'd done and shaming the family. Don frantically apologized and promised never to do it again, but he got a good taste of what it feels like to drown before his father was satisfied.

. . . .

Mike had been so preoccupied with Don's temper that he stopped paying attention to the road.

Suddenly, he frowned, looking out the window. "Whatta we doin' here?"

Don coasted through the parking lot, without saying a word, until he eased into the furthest corner and parked.

Mike's body stiffened.

He forgot about his pain and slipped into survival mode.

"Get out," said Don.

"Huh?"

"I said get out."

"Why?"

"So you can walk to the damn doctor yourself."

"What the hell's the deal?"

"I said, get out—now!"

Mike grimaced, but the corresponding pain to his nose put him in check.

Irritated, he threw open the car door and stepped out, refusing to acknowledge Don's glower.

"Don't forget our conversation," said Don.

Mike slammed the door and started walking.

Don made a slow U-turn, keeping his eyes on Mike the whole time. Then he slammed on the gas and drove back to town.

Chapter 4

At Fosters Bighorn Antonio and John stared at the beer in front of them.

"You sure you don't need a doctor?" said Stacey.

"I'll be fine," said John.

"I shouldn't have hit him so hard," said Antonio.

"Forget it," said John. "It wasn't your fault."

"It's just that . . . I hate when things like that happen."

"I can't believe you still have it in you. I guess Special Forces training really does run through your veins."

"Maybe too much," said Stacey.

"Relax," said John. "We're here to decompress. Don't start getting down on me—neither of you. How 'bout another round?"

John caught the bartender's attention.

"You know," Antonio clasped his hands. "I'll never forget the way you took care of my brother while I was in Korea."

John took a swig. "It wasn't such a selfless act, you know."

"But you really took care of him. That's the thing."

"What else could we've done? We were convinced we'd never have kids of our own—at least not until Gary came along. And what a better deal than to adopt someone we already loved. Trust me, nothing could've made us happier."

"I'll never forget it, John."

"I know." He took another drink.

"Well," said Stacey, "I guess you feel proud of yourself—beating up on Mike."

"Cut it out," said John. "I told you it wasn't his fault."

She took a gulp of her margarita, having to swallow twice to get it all down.

"I'm sorry," she said. "I guess I'm still upset. And this talk about Korea isn't helping much. I don't like it."

"Neither do I," said Antonio.

"Then why are we talking about it?"

"Because no matter how much I wanna put it behind me, it's still part of my life. You think I like remembering that I lost you because of it?"

She took another gulp.

The memory of Stacey backing away slowly with the horror of betrayal in her face still made Antonio shudder.

"What do you mean, you're leaving?" she said.

Antonio's eyes clenched.

He had hoped for understanding and a semblance of peace. After all, if his plan seemed rash, it was only because his parents' death had been so sudden.

"I need to provide for my brother," he said. "Besides, we might not get into the same school, and you and I will be separated anyway."

"It's not the same thing, and you know it."

"Look, it's only four years. Then the Army'll pay for my school, and Rubén'll be in college. He'll be able to take care of himself at that point."

She shook her head. "What if something happens to you?"

"Nothing's gonna happen."

"How do you know?"

"Well, what if something happens to me here?" said Antonio, anticipating a dead-end conversation.

"It's not the same thing."

"I need to take care of my brother. That's all there is to it."

"So you don't care what I think?"

Antonio reached out to her, but she pulled back. "That's not what I said. You just need to let me take care of my brother. He's all the family I have left. And I'll never get a second chance. He needs me."

"Help him from here."

"Doing what?" said Antonio. "Packing grocery bags?"

Her eyes welled up with frustration.

"The Army didn't make me who I am, Stacey—if that's what you're thinking. All they taught me was how to fight and survive." Antonio winced at the thought. "It was my brother who helped me become a man. He's the reason I survived. He's what kept me going and made me wanna come back." He took a deep breath. "I'm not gonna lie. There *were* times—after seeing some of my friends die— that I just wanted to be next. That demilitarized zone is nothing pretty. But it finally sunk in that Rubén was gonna need me sane when I got back, and I wanted to give him the best of what I knew my parents would've given him."

Stacey remained silent.

"You did," she said, finally.

"I just wish they'd seen him graduate."

"I'm sure they did," said John, "in their own way."

With a feeble smile Antonio drank from his beer.

. . . .

John insisted on another round of drinks.

Meanwhile, Antonio caught Stacey glancing at his shoulders.

"How do you stay so fit?" she said. "Most priests I know start getting chubby after a while."

"Working on the farm in Mexico, I guess. I helped out as often as I could. And I try to keep up with my running. What about you?"

"It's actually not that difficult for me. Work and exercise are my only distractions."

"Oh, come on!" said Antonio.

"Really. Think about it." She stared into empty space. "All my friends are gone. Even my parents moved to Sacramento."

"Why are *you* still here?"

"Don—he never did wanna leave. I respected his wishes, but I had to work my career around his. Now here I am, principal of Rio Vista High School." She tried to smile. "At least I'm not stuck anymore. I'm really looking forward to a superintendent opening in Sacramento."

"That's excellent!"

"I've just been lucky that I can count on someone like John, while I'm still here."

"I'll drink to that," said John. "You're the best this town has to offer." He raised his beer in front of him. "When you go to Sacramento, you're gonna have to take me with you."

"If it's up to me, you'll be there the same day I am. I don't know what I'd do without you. You've been my only support."

"Don't talk like that."

"It's true. Except for Don's mom, actually. She's such a sweetheart. She always did so much to try and help us. Treated me like her own daughter. She's suffered so much, though. That family doesn't know how to appreciate her."

"And that husband of hers," said John. "Don's turning out just like him."

"No kidding. Don has everyone believing I'm some sort of self-serving wench—just because I left him. He sees himself as a public figure now, you see. I don't know what he's done to make some people believe in him. He's cleaned up the town really well, but you saw how he does it."

"Be careful when you run into him," John told Antonio. "He'll have an eye out for you."

"Yeah, he let me know." Antonio snickered. "Don't worry. I don't have a whole lot to say to him."

"I'm so glad I never had kids," said Stacey. "Things would be so much more complicated. I really wanted to for a while. He never did—at least not at the beginning. I guess it all turned out for the better. The only sad thing is that it's getting too late for me now."

"There's plenty of time," said John

"Not really."

"Look, why don't we all go away for the weekend and celebrate our reunion?"

"Where?" said Stacey.

"Who cares. Let's just get away and relax."

Stacey turned to Antonio. "Whatta you think?"

"Well, that would be nice, except that I just got a job with Jack."

"Your dad's old boss?" said John.

"Yeah, his son. My old classmate, remember? I don't think I should run out on him so soon. I don't have much else going for me right now."

"Oooh," John mocked, "and what are we? Decorations?"

Antonio grinned. "You know what I mean." He stared at his beer. "I need to start taking care of a few things."

Stacey reached over and laid her hand on Antonio's.

"I'll be right back," said John. "I have to use the restroom."

He got up and sauntered away as Antonio watched in disbelief.

"I'm really glad you came," said Stacey. "I thought I might never see you again."

She smiled as they caught each other's eye.

Antonio glanced away.

"What's wrong?" said Stacey.

"I wasn't sure how I'd feel when I saw you." He sensed her waiting for more. "I don't really know what else to say right now."

"That's okay. Time'll tell us everything."

He tried to conceal a half-hearted smile.

"What is it?" said Stacey.

"I just don't want old feelings to interfere with doing the right thing."

"I know what I'm doing."

"But do you *still* know me?" He questioned the sharpness of his tone.

"Of course, I know you. I know everything that's happened to you, and I want to be here for you. John always made sure I saw your letters. He knew I wasn't happy."

"You don't know what happened right before I left Mexico."

"I know something didn't work out. Otherwise, you wouldn't be here."

"I'm still planning to finish the priesthood, Stacey. It's just that something happened, and I might have to finish here, instead of Mexico." He squeezed her hand. "You're a good woman. Things will work out for you."

"I wish I'd been stronger when you were in Korea."

"We can't worry about that now."

"I let people convince me you wouldn't make it back—and that I needed something different."

"Why?" said Antonio. "Because I was a poor farm boy?"

"Partly."

"What other reason could there have been?"

"My parents didn't think you were too bright for giving up on school and going to fight a pointless war."

An awkward silence ensued.

"Nothing's changed. I'm still poor. And it would seem that I'm still fighting pointless wars."

"Well, I've outgrown all that. You made me stronger—the same way you said your brother made *you* stronger. I learned to fight for what I want." She paused. "What's sad is that . . . I think my initial failure to fight for *our* relationship is what made me fight for my relationship with Don." Her eyes welled up. "I didn't want my lack of effort to be a factor again. I felt so guilty about what happened to *us*. I just wanted to be happy."

Antonio patted her hand. "God provides, Stacey. Just not always the way we want or expect."

They saw John coming back.

Stacey blinked hard and fast, wiping the overflow from her left eye.

"There we go," said John. He sat down and lifted his beer. "Here's to a great weekend."

"To my having found a job," said Antonio.

"Oh, yeah, that too." John smiled. "I think we're gonna need a ride after this."

"Most definitely," said Stacey, and they toasted again.

When they finished their drinks, they asked Brian if he was leaving any time soon. He said he was fine to drive, and he could give them a ride as soon as he took care of his tab.

They put on their jackets and walked out together—chuckling the whole way.

When John squatted down for a stretch, his knees protested. Antonio had to help him up.

They squeezed into Brian's back seat with Stacey in the middle.

"God, it's cold," said Stacey, exhaling a warm, misty breath. "You can drop me off at Maplewood apartments."

"Why are you staying there?" said Antonio.

"I didn't wanna argue with Don about the house, so I just moved out."

"You guys know what time it is?" John asked.

"Eleven-ten," said Stacey.

John squeezed his eyes shut. "Uh! Don't wake me up before eight."

"Come on, John. You have a guest. Tomorrow's a special day. Surely, you can make an exception."

"Exception, my butt. If I don't sleep, there won't be anything special about it."

Stacey laughed, knowingly, with Antonio.

"It's not my fault. That's just the way my body works."

"We know," said Stacey. "Don't worry."

Before they knew it, Brian pulled into the apartment complex.

"I guess I'll see you guys tomorrow." Stacey hugged John.

Antonio opened the door and stepped out.

Stacey dug into her purse, trying to pay John for her share of the drinks.

"I told you not to worry about it."

"No, that's okay."

"Stacey, it's taken care of."

"Oh, all right."

She hugged John again, giving him a big kiss on the cheek. Stepping out of the car, she kissed Antonio softly on his cheek.

"I'll see you tomorrow," she said.

"Goodnight."

Antonio waited until she walked up to her second-floor apartment. They waved good-bye as she went inside.

Antonio turned and leaned over the car door.

"Let's walk home," he said.

John looked up from inside. "Are you crazy?"

"Come on, John. It's not that bad."

"It's farther than heck."

"It's not that far. Besides, we could use the exercise."

"I don't need any exercise."

"Come on. I'm tired of sitting. It's not that bad."

"Ah, hell," said John, stepping out of the car.

They thanked Brian.

"If I get sick, I'm holding you responsible," said John.

"Don't worry. You won't get sick. But if you do, think of it as retribution for all you made me suffer during those track and cross-country seasons."

"Don't give me that crap."

"What's the matter, John? Not happy to see me anymore?"

Antonio threw his arm around John's shoulder as they walked along.

They woke a dog across the street. It barked in protest.

"Sounds like we're waking up the neighborhood," said Antonio.

"What kind of job you gonna be doing for Jack?"

"Just some odds and ends for a few weeks—until his guy comes back."

"Then what?"

"I've gotta call the diocese—to let them know what happened and see if I can transfer up here. I'm not sure what they'll say, but I need to find out."

"Are you sure that's what you want?"

"Of course, I'm sure."

The chill numbed their face as they thumped their way down the sidewalk.

John's weight shifted slightly to one side. Antonio had to pull him back.

"Careful," he said, "you're gonna knock us both over."

"Sorry."

John's house lay right on the bank of the Sacramento River.

A huge redwood towered over the front lawn, while a half-barren maple stood next to it with fallen, rusty leaves illuminated by the porch light.

Upon entering the house, Antonio drank a full glass of water to avoid a headache.

John showed him to the guestroom, and they wished each other a good night.

Chapter 5

Antonio woke up around five in the morning. After some prayer and reflection, he raided the closet for something to run in, lucking out with some old swim trunks and a sweatshirt. He took his time sipping on a glass of water at the kitchen counter, then grabbed John's car keys and jogged down to the marina, toward the outskirts of town.

The lingering cold took some getting used to. Even after warming up, his face remained numb, and the fog hardly showed signs of relenting.

He took Montezuma Hills Road and turned onto Emigh—better known to the cross-country team as the roller coaster run. He ran out as far as the Amerada Hess Petroleum Company. Upon finding the fenced entrance closed, he turned back, reminiscing over all the practice runs he and Jack had suffered through together—not to mention all the shoes they must have worn out on that road alone.

And the beer run! He could never forget the beer run. They had completely given new meaning to the phrase. After all, how often do a couple of teenagers find a six pack of beer, just begging to be consumed, lying on the side of the road, while jogging?

He still found it hard to believe.

Someone must've panicked about getting caught and dumped it, so he and Jack grabbed the goods, ran to the cover of the nearest gas well, and worked on acquiring a new taste.

An interesting day, to say the least.

Antonio breathed deeply. And every breath seemed to bring back memories.

When he got back to town, he ran up to where they had parked the night before. He wondered how Stacey was doing as he warmed up John's car.

His thoughts took him back to grammar school—and his initial attraction to Stacey. She used to wear eyeglasses and straight, brown hair of medium length. They made her look rather plain, but her firm posture easily made up for it. That's why he always picked her to be on his soccer team during recess.

She was so quiet back then. And it took him years to overcome his own shyness. In fact, he couldn't remember having a good conversation with her until they were already in high school.

He put the car in gear and drove back to John's house.

Once parked, he grabbed his duffel bag and the Saturday morning newspaper. He went inside and took a shower.

By six-thirty he was back in the kitchen—clean shaven—wearing an old pair of pants, a discolored long-sleeve shirt, and work boots. He started making *torta de huevo* with *chile* and some oatmeal for breakfast.

He took some leftovers from the refrigerator and warmed them up as well.

When the phone rang, he picked it up quickly to avoid waking John.

"I knew you'd be awake," said Stacey.

"You just wake up?"

"No, about an hour ago."

"Is everything okay?"

"Yeah. I was just wondering if you'd like to go out for a picnic later."

"I don't know what time I'll be back from work."

"You can give me a call."

"It might be late."

"That's okay. We'll make it dinner."

Antonio poured himself a glass of orange juice.

"Yeah, that sounds all right."

"Okay. I'm gonna pick up my car. I'll talk to you later."

"Let me drive over and give you a lift."

"That's all right. I need the walk."

"You sure?"

"Positive."

Antonio hung up and drank from his orange juice. He finished boiling the oatmeal and took a stool at the breakfast bar to read the newspaper. In the sunken living room stood the grand piano that John used to play for his late wife, Beth.

Above the fireplace hung John and Beth's wedding picture. Another of Gary's high school graduation hung to one side, with Antonio and Rubén on the other. It was a pleasant house. Everything had its place and not much traffic to bring about imbalance.

John walked into the living room, squinting at Antonio. "So what's going on?"

Antonio smiled. "You look like a mess this morning."

"Thanks. I'm gonna shower. Is everything okay?"

"Everything's fine. How's your arm?"

"Could be worse, I guess."

As John withdrew, Antonio put the newspaper aside and finished cooking the *torta de huevo* with *chile*. He loved cooking on weekends. It relaxed and helped him forget his troubles.

He was almost done eating when John, once again, emerged.

"I'm glad you're still alive," said Antonio.

"So am I." He shuffled to the kitchen. "That smells like a heck of a breakfast. Just what I need for this dang hangover."

"It's *torta de huevo con chile*."

"Excellent!"

John grabbed a plate with his left hand and winced. His forearm was noticeably swollen and purple.

"You need some help?" said Antonio.

"I'll be fine." He set the plate on the stove and served himself with his right hand.

"That arm's pretty swollen. I hope you showered with cold water. You sure you don't wanna see a doctor?"

"No. I'll just put some ice on it later." He carefully set his left arm on the table before sitting down. "You know why I was so happy to be buzzed last night?"

"Why's that?"

He tried to flex his arm and cackled. "'Cause I knew my arm would be hurting like a son-of-a-gun as soon as I sobered up."

Antonio shook his head with a smile.

"You were up early this morning," said John.

"I told you I had a job to go to."

"You should relax a couple of days."

"I can't. I need to keep myself busy. Otherwise, I'll go crazy."

"You still haven't told me exactly what happened in Mexico."

"I have to get going. It's already late."

John scowled. "Bullcrap! You're not gonna pull that again."

Antonio gave him a prolonged gaze before taking a deep breath. "But you can't tell Stacey. I'd rather tell her myself."

"Fine. I can deal with that."

"Well," he gathered his thoughts, "remember I told you about the foremen on the neighboring farm?"

"Yeah."

"They pretty much had it in for me once I started helping the workers address their working conditions." He sat up straight. "They were heartless taskmasters. And they hated the fact that I showed more respect for the workers than I did for them—although that was purely incidental."

"So what happened?"

"One of the foremen filled the farm owner's head with rumors about my having messed with his daughter and getting her pregnant. That's when things got really crazy. My best guess is that it was the foreman himself who had a thing going with the daughter, and when she ended up pregnant, he needed an excuse to not lose his job and get rid of me at the same time. Not surprisingly, he offered to marry the daughter and save her from public scrutiny. By this point, the folks at the seminary were pretty concerned. They were in the process of transferring me somewhere else, but I kept trying to help the workers as much as I could before I left. Then, a couple of weeks ago, one of the foremen was found dead."

John's eyes opened wide. "What the hell?"

"I had just met with the workers. The foreman must've been spying on me. He confronted me with a knife on my way home. All I did was defend myself. I didn't even hurt him that much. I just left him recovering out in the field. The only thing I can figure is that someone saw what happened and bashed him up after I left. All the foremen blamed me, of course. And I had no choice but to run. I didn't stand a chance. The Church would've helped me with a lawyer, but I don't think that would've made much of a difference." He poked his food with a fork. "Anyway, things got really complicated, and I had to leave."

"I can imagine."

"But you know what?" said Antonio. "I could deal with all of that. What really gets me is how people can mess with others' lives so mindlessly. And I'm not talking about me. I mean the guys I was trying to help." Antonio stuffed his mouth with the last of his breakfast. "So here I am," he mumbled. "What I need to do is call some priests I know—see if they can help me sort things out, like I told you."

John nodded.

"I've gotta go. I'll talk to you later."

"Take the car," said John.

"I can take the bike. It's only four miles."

"Take the car, or I'll drive you myself."

Chapter 6

The morning sun struggled to burn through the remaining fog on the bank of the Sacramento River. As they left the house a lingering frigidity pierced John and Antonio, with the reminder that winter had indeed asserted itself. The redwood tree in the front yard remained majestic and unaffected, while the unpruned maple stood skeleton-like, with the sun cutting through its branches.

They drove down Front Street and onto the Rio Vista Bridge, as Antonio contemplated its twin lift towers, looming in the morning brightness. He lowered his window to receive a dose of fresh air. On either side of the bridge, the sun began to sparkle amidst the waves, while a sweeping flight of red-winged black birds inspired a sigh of appreciation. He knew he couldn't be anywhere else at that moment, except the River Delta, and his yearning again went out to years gone by.

As they passed the apple orchard, Antonio noticed that the gas well on their left remained active. Highway Twelve was already bustling with traffic, and tractors began to run up and down the corn-stubbled fields, cultivating them for the next crop of wheat.

John took a left on Jackson Slough Road, before turning onto the gravel road entrance, where a worker was hitching a tractor and harrow.

The car coasted all the way to the tractor shop.

When Antonio emerged, he welcomed the fortifying petrichor of the open fields.

As he waved good-bye to John, he recognized the huge walnut tree, still hovering over the tractor shop, with its leaves weather-stained to a rusty yellow and starting to shed. Farm equipment lay scattered about like an open graveyard, while the corn harvester next to the shop waited to be put away for the winter.

Scoping around, Antonio was caught off guard by a black bull staring at him from next to the old redwood shed that now struggled to hold itself up under the apricot tree.

They fixed their sights on one another.

When neither budged, Antonio staged a jerking stoop with outstretched arms, as if for balance.

The bull flinched, lifting its enormous neck and turning to the calm of its shed.

Antonio relished the moment before approaching the man on the harrow.

"*Rogelio*," he said. "*¿donde está Jack?*"

Rogelio pointed. "*Está mecaniquiando en el chop.*"

"*Gracias.*"

Antonio sauntered over to the shop, where Jack Smith struggled on his knees to replace a tractor starter. He was a stalky fellow, blond and permanently sunbaked in the face and arms. He wore what appeared to be blue jeans, a long-sleeve t-shirt, and an old sweatshirt with cut-off sleeves that must have belonged to his father and grandfather before him. The dirt floor was stained black with oil, as was the workbench behind him.

"Let me give you a hand," said Antonio.

Jack swung around, supporting himself on the huge tractor tire. "Hell, I was startin' ta worry. Help me out here so I can show ya around."

Antonio began rolling up his sleeves.

"There's a pair of overalls up on the tractor seat," said Jack.

Antonio went to grab it.

When he opened the tractor door, the familiar smell of diesel engine and dirt gripped him. He saw the hydraulic levers and realized it was the same Steiger tractor his father had driven when he was young. Occasionally, his father would take him to work on weekends, and he'd sit proudly at his father's right flank, imagining what it would be like when he drove one himself.

He grabbed the overalls and slipped them on.

"When are you getting a new tractor, Jack? This is the same one from when we were kids, isn't it?"

"Hey," came the voice from under the tractor, "don't start harassin' me so early. These things ain't cheap, ya know. And farmin' aint what it used ta be. We used ta farm everything, remember? Now you'd think all we eat is wheat and corn. Competin' with those mega-farmers isn't gettin' any easier."

Antonio jumped off the tractor.

"Remember when I fell off this thing and split my head open?"

"Yeah!" Jack howled. "You had ta wear that stupid-lookin' bandage on your head."

"At least I didn't break my neck."

"How 'bout that scar on your back—from when our tree house collapsed? Ya still have it?"

"Yup, still there."

Antonio ducked under the tractor and held the starter in place, while Jack finished unbolting it. It felt good to work with his hands again.

Outside, someone honked their way into the gravel road entrance.

Antonio turned and saw John's car driving back in. It blared one last honk before coming to a stop.

"Hold on a second, Jack."

"Tell whoever that is ta stop honkin'. They're gonna spook my bull. Did ya see him when you came in?"

"Yeah." Antonio came out from under the tractor, zipping up his overall and leaning against the large, sliding door.

John leaned over the passenger seat to grab something.

He threw open the door and worked his way out.

"You forgot your jacket," he said, plodding toward Antonio.

Antonio acknowledged with a nod and went to meet him.

John walked heavily, holding his injured arm close to his side.

That's when the bull reemerged from behind the old shed. It observed John bouncing along, with the coat dangling in front of him.

Tantalized, the bull instinctively lowered its head and snorted. Then it waved its head in the air, as if to make a show of its horns.

It snorted again.

When Rogelio looked up, John turned in horror.

"Be careful," said Rogelio. "Don' move." He waved his hands in the air from atop the harrow, trying to get the bull's attention. "He don' like strangers."

John froze as the bull struck its hoof on the ground.

Antonio also waved his hands in the air, but not before the bull struck its hoof one last time and charged forward.

John lost his sense of perception. Instead of retreating back to the safety of his car, he tried to scamper forward toward the shop. He took two clumsy steps and tumbled, falling to his knees and then his stomach.

"Jack!" Rogelio yelled, as he jumped off the harrow.

Antonio saw the bull in full gallop and sprang forward.

With a tight grip in his gut, he dashed with adrenaline, taking several measured strides. As he was about to collide with the bull, he leaped onto its neck and grabbed its horns.

The bull yanked its head, trying to toss him.

Antonio leveraged his body against the bull's shoulder, twisting and pulling its horns to the side and back onto its neck.

Its massive body crashed with the momentum, tumbling over with a loud thump.

The bull gasped in horror, wide-eyed and motionless.

Antonio bounced up and went to see after John.

"You okay?" said Antonio.

John had broken into a cold sweat, staring at Antonio without recognition.

The bull finally got to its feet and trotted back to the shed.

"Damn!" gaped Jack. He saw everything from the shop. "How the hellja do that?"

"He's in shock," said Antonio. "Help me out."

Antonio yanked the jacket from John's hands and laid it over him. Then he took off his overalls and covered him with those as well.

Rogelio ran off. "I get water."

"Should I call for help?" said Jack.

John shook his head, struggling to reestablish his grip on reality.

"I think he's coming around," said Antonio.

Rogelio returned with a pail of water.

Antonio dipped his hand and wiped it across John's pallid face several times.

After a moment, John raised his head and sat up, still shaking.

"How'd you get 'm off me?" he said.

"Don't worry. You're okay." Antonio smiled, trying to calm him down. "Look, you didn't even drop my jacket. It's still clean."

He pulled on one of the sleeves to show him. John tried to smile, and color started flowing back into his face.

"Ya sure you're okay?" said Jack.

"I'm alright," he said, but a frown abruptly took over. "What the hell's the deal with the bull?"

"Oh, . . . he's . . . kind o' my watchdog around here."

"Watch dog?" The shock in John's eyes turned to anger. "You're gonna get someone killed." He tried to get up, but fell back to his knees.

"Actually, he's tied up most o' the time," said Jack. "I'm really sorry."

Antonio offered John a hand and helped him up.

John winced at the pain in his arm.

"You sure you can drive?" said Jack.

"I'm fine," he snapped. "You better keep that damn thing leashed."

"Ya don't wanna sit down for a while?"

"No! I don't."

John handed Antonio his jacket and overalls before stammering back to the car and driving off in a frenzy.

. . . .

"You wanna tie up that bull?" said Antonio.

"Yeah. Don't know what came over 'm. And Mr. Keefe of all people. How the hellja do that, anyway?"

"What? The bull?"

"Yeah—the bull."

"I just twisted its neck. It's their vulnerable spot."

Jack gave him a slanted look. "It's that easy, huh? They teach you that in seminary too?"

"No. I saw an old man do it in Korea."

"Old man?"

"Well, he was in his late fifties, but you'd never know it. He was one of my *tae kwon do* instructors."

"Really? I was talkin' ta Anne about that once, and we honestly couldn't figure out how you made it into the Special Forces."

Antonio shrugged. "I guess they figured I liked pain, so they encouraged me to join the rest of the pain lovers—see if I could hack it."

They walked behind the dilapidated shed, where they found the bull still panting and giving off heavy clouds of breath. It looked disoriented as it considered them with caution. Jack approached it slowly, caressing and patting its neck and shoulder.

"He's all right," said Jack.

"How the heck did you end up with a bull for a watchdog, anyway?"

Jack picked up the end of a rope that was tied to a stake and adjusted the loop around the bull's horns.

"Come 'ere," said Jack. "His name's Max. Pet 'm so he can get used ta you."

Antonio put his hand on the bull's jaw and petted.

"I got 'm when he was just a calf. A friend o' mine works at a dairy stable, and they give 'em away when they're born with birth defects." He squatted down at the bull's front legs. "See the scars on his joints? He was crippled. The tendons behind his hoofs were too tight. They wouldn't let his legs straighten out, so he moved around like he was crawlin'. We had ta tie some boards on the front side of his hoof joints ta force 'em little by little."

Antonio's eyebrows went up. "Why didn't you get a normal dog?"

Jack stood up. "Well, we didn't expect 'm ta grow so fast. He was supposed ta be a pet for my son—a birthday present. He said that's what he wanted. I figured we could eat 'm when he got bigger. But, hell, you can't eat a pet."

"How old are the kids now?"

"Jill's seven. Gavin's eight."

"I guess you and Anne took care of business after I left. I wasn't sure if you'd even get married."

"I know. So many break-ups. I find it hard ta believe myself. It hasn't been *all* pretty, but I wouldn't change it for nothin'."

"I guess you have to act when the moment's right."

"Pretty much," said Jack. "What about you? Any interesting ladies?"

"All the time," Antonio jested, as he examined the shed. One of the walls had been torn out so the bull could use it as shelter. "Just can't do anything about it."

"What about—" Jack stopped himself.

"What?"

"Nothin'."

Antonio gave the bull one last pat on the shoulder.

As they came around the shed, Antonio bumped the bottom corner with his boot and shook the entire structure. When he looked up, he noticed thick moss deposits on the roof.

"When are you gonna tear this thing down?" said Antonio.

"Tear it down? Are you kiddin'? Where am I gonna put Max?"

"I can build you a new one. I bet your son would appreciate it."

"You got that right. He loves that bull. Too bad he's too big ta play with anymore."

"How does it feel to be a dad, anyway?"

"Pretty damn frustrating sometimes."

"Well, yeah. But you know what I mean."

"Nothin' like it," said Jack. "I still can't believe they're my kids sometimes."

Antonio's eyes brightened up. "It must be the greatest feeling in the world, knowing that—hey—these are *my* kids? That they're a part of you—a product of you, even."

Jack's eyes widened. "You're freakin' me out, buddy. You seem pretty intimate with this feelin'."

Antonio laughed. "I'm just remembering my brother's kids. Maybe it's because he's my only brother, but seeing them was like nothing I've ever felt before. When they called me *tio*, I just wanted to scoop them up and squeeze them to no end."

"I'm telling ya, it's not as pretty as you make it sound."

"Of course. But that goes with everything, right? Everything that's worthwhile takes time and effort."

"Exactly," said Jack.

. . . .

Florescent lamps illuminated the inside of the shop, while Jack and Antonio finished replacing the tractor starter. Things had gone slowly with much talk and little work. When they finally emerged from under the tractor, they degreased their hands in the concrete sink at the back of the shop.

"By the way," said Jack, "Anne was pretty upset 'cause I didn't bring ya over yesterday, after we talked about you helping out around here, so I want ya ta know that I blamed it all on you."

"What'd she say?"

"She told me I had to bring you tonight."

Antonio winced. "I'll have to talk to Stacey. I told her I'd meet up with her for dinner."

"So you *are* seein' her!"

"No!" said Antonio. "I'm just having dinner with her."

"Hell, why is it women always have ta come between us? What about lunch?"

"That works."

"Great!" said Jack. "I'll give Anne a call. Just don't forget— we still have ta go out 'n celebrate."

Antonio cringed. "Celebrate?"

"Yeah, celebrate! Ya know—as in go out 'n have a couple drinks."

"I was afraid you'd say that."

"What? You gettin' soft on me?"

"I don't know if I can handle it right now, Jack. I had a few last night."

He glared at Antonio. "Whattaya mean *last night*?"

"I went out and had some drinks with John and Stacey."

"Well, shit. That's your problem for not invitin' me."

"Sorry, Jack. It was spur of the moment."

"I don't give a damn if it was spur o' the moment or not."

"Don't worry. You didn't miss anything—anything good at least. Just some damn kid trying to pick a fight."

Jack caught his breath. "You ain't talkin' about the ruckus at Foster's last night, are ya?"

"Yeah."

"With Don's nephew?"

"Yeah—Mike. How'd you know?"

"Holly shit!" Jack's face lit up. "You ain't the guy that caused the problems there last night, are ya?"

"No! I was part of it, but I didn't *cause* the problem."

"That's not what's goin' around."

"Why? What's going around?"

Jack's face suddenly reflected pain. "Shit! I can't believe I missed it."

"What?"

"Nothin'."

"Wha'd you hear?"

"That this crazy guy was talkin' crap about Don and his nephew. Supposedly, the kid tried ta defend himself and got his nose broke."

"I was with John Keefe," said Antonio. "You think he would've just let something like that happen?"

"I'm not sayin' I believe it. That's just what I heard."

"Did they say anything about John?"

"No."

Antonio shook his head. "Mike almost broke his arm."

"Are you serious? Is he okay?"

"He says he is, but that's why he looked like he was in pain before he left."

"Hell, Don's probably burnin' with rage now that you're back. I bet that's why Stacey's name was slapped all over the place. You said she was with ya, right?"

"Yeah—and John."

"That's why he's tryin' to make a big stink outta this. I was wonderin' what it was all about. Didn't I tell ya he was a little bastard?"

"How'd you find out, anyway?"

"I'm sure Don got his little gossip network workin' overtime last night. I heard from Bowers. He called me late last night."

"I think I'm starting to understand what Stacey's been going through."

"Yeah, it definitely stinks."

"Isn't there something we can do to stop this?"

"Don't worry. We'll think o' somethin'."

After grabbing their jacket and turning off the florescent lights, Jack closed the sliding door to the tractor shop behind them.

The yellow fog light remained lit over the shop itself.

"You gonna turn that one off," said Antonio.

"No. That one stays on all the time."

Jack locked the sliding door and gave Antonio a duplicate key.

. . . .

Anne was waiting eagerly at the house with lunch already prepared when Jack and Antonio arrived. She hadn't seen Antonio in nine years, and she received him as if it were twenty. She wanted to know everything. No excuses. And Antonio was more than happy to oblige, only hesitating when she asked why he came back. But even that he confessed—just not with the same enthusiasm. In the end, he was glad to get it out of the way.

Jack and Antonio had already cleaned up before arriving, but Anne made them wash their hands again before eating. She didn't want the kids catching anything. She ran a clean shop, and she meant to keep it that way.

"I can see why Jack's such a happy guy," said Antonio.

Anne offered her two cents. "You know it's your fault I married this madman, don't you?"

"Madman?" said Jack.

"Okay—this darling madman."

Jack frowned. "I guess that's better."

"He was so jealous when I told him I used to have a crush on you."

"I was not."

"Yes, you were. Besides, what's there to be upset about? We never even kissed."

"I don't wanna talk about this in front o' the kids."

"The kids?" She looked at one and then the other. "There's nothing to worry about, is there, kids? If it weren't for uncle Antonio, here, your dad and I would probably never have married, and you wouldn't be here." The kids gave each other a blank look. "First of all, he told me I wasn't his type. Then he kept telling me about his wonderful friend, whose name just happened to be Jack."

The kids giggled this time.

"She has some way with the kids," said Jack.

"I can see that," said Antonio.

"Hey, Gavin," Jack tried to change the subject, "we were thinkin' about tearin' down the old shed and buildin' a new one for Max."

"Why?"

"Well, uncle Antonio thinks it might fall down 'n hurt Max."

"But won't he get sick? It's been raining."

"Oh, I hadn't even thought o' that."

"We can put him in the tractor shop," Antonio suggested.

"Yeah, that's a good idea," said Jack.

"Okay," Gavin agreed. "But only if it doesn't take too long?"

"It shouldn't take more than a week." Jack elbowed Antonio. "Looks like we're gonna be workin' some overtime."

"That's fine with me. I could use the distraction."

"Good."

"In fact," said Antonio, "maybe we could build it on a concrete foundation this time—make sure we never have to worry about it again."

"That just means more work."

"I'm up for it." Antonio turned to Gavin. "Maybe we can turn it into a regular mansion."

"Yeeeah!" said Gavin, his eyes wide open.

"Wait a second," said Jack. "Let's not get carried away here. That money's comin' out of *my* pocket."

"Well, you don't have to worry about paying me the overtime. I'd be more than happy to do it for Gavin."

Anne smiled.

"You sure?" said Jack.

"Absolutely."

"Cooool!" Gavin's face beamed with satisfaction. "Can I go out and play now?"

Jill joined the plea. "Me too, mommy."

"Okay," said Anne. "You ate pretty well."

They ran to the door as fast as they could, pushing each other for space.

"You have beautiful kids," said Antonio.

"Which one?" said Jack.

Anne smacked him on the shoulder. "Whatta you trying to say?"

"Just that girls are more adorable—that's all."

"Well, don't let Gavin hear you say that. You'll hurt his feelings."

"Oh, come on, Anne. You know me better than that."

Antonio delighted in their exchange. "Kids *are* beautiful, though."

"Well," Jack remarked, "it'd be great if they didn't have ta grow up. Other than that, I'd have to agree that they're the closest thing ta heaven."

"*Almas de Dios*," Antonio concurred. "A reflection of God's soul—at least the innocent side of them."

"I think you guys ate too much," said Anne.

"Why?" said Jack. "Just because Antonio has an over-romanticized idea of parenting 'n kids? Don't you remember when the kids were younger?"

"What about it?"

"You said I seemed like a different person."

"Oh, that."

"I even started treatin' other people different, you said. And your mom said she was startin' ta like me, remember?"

"Okay, okay, I guess kids do have that effect on you."

The arguing squeals of Gavin and Jill suddenly drifted in from outside.

"So much for that," said Anne.

Jill cried as she ran into the house and began to pout, with tears streaming down her cheeks.

Anne received her with open arms. "What's the matter, honey?"

"Gavin hit me."

"Too bad it all comes to an end," said Anne.

CHAPTER 7

Don parked his gray BMW and stepped out, wearing freshly pressed slacks, a white shirt, and a tie. He observed the house in front of him, then walked up the wooden steps and onto the porch. He rang the doorbell and waited. Although one of the nicer-looking homes in the neighborhood, it had taken thirty years of effort to get there. Somewhat lacking in architectural integrity, it had started as a simple box-like structure when barged in at a bargain price from one of the neighboring islands in the River Delta. As time went by, contractors added the front porch, the dining room addition to the side, the room in the back, and finally, the garage and driveway on the left.

A stubby, yet sturdy man with gray hair and sharp features opened the front door and looked at Don.

"Hey, dad," said Don, extending his arm to shake hands.

Craig Lacey stared for a second before accepting.

"Where're you goin'?"

"Nowhere. Just thought I'd come an' see you."

Craig narrowed his brows and grunted.

"What're you up to today?" said Don.

"Nothin'. There ain't nothin' to be up to."

"You ain't workin' on someone's car this weekend?"

Craig's tone became sharp. "I told you I'm tired o' that crap. Been doin' the same thing since before you were born. I'm takin' it easy now that I don't have ta take care o' nobody. And I finally got rid o' Tim, too. Kept sayin' he was broke. The damn divorce cost 'm too much. Thought he'as never gonna leave."

"Yeah, he told me." Don craned his neck to look inside. "Where's mom?"

"Upstairs somewhere."

"Can I come in?"

"Sure."

Don stepped in, leaning against the staircase railing that led up to the second floor. "Hey, mom!" he yelled. "Where you at?"

"Hi, Don. I'll be right down," she hollered back.

Don walked into the living room and took a seat on the couch below the wall mirror. The television was on college football—UCLA vs. USC. Don crossed his legs and observed his dad.

Craig leaned back on his recliner, drinking from his beer and cursing at the television.

"Who's winning?" said Don.

"UCLA."

Don heard dull thumps coming down the staircase. He stood up as his mother, Sharon Lacey, tottered into the living room. She was short and wide, with eyes that sagged almost painfully.

"Hi, son," she said, giving Don a hug. "It's sure nice to see you. It's been a while."

"How're you, mom?"

"Fine. Sit down. You want anything to drink?"

"How 'bout a beer?"

"Sure, let me get it for you."

He sat down.

Sharon made her way to the kitchen.

The game was on second down, and USC was on UCLA's four-yard line.

"Come on you son-of-a-bitches," said Craig.

"They don't stand a chance."

"What the hell would you know?" said Craig, keeping his eyes on the television.

"They've been struggling all season."

"So. That don't mean crap. This is a rivalry game."

Don heard his mother calling from the kitchen. "Don, you want a glass for your beer?"

"No. That's fine."

"Damn!" said Craig.

Sharon emerged from the kitchen. She handed Don his beer and sat on the couch next to him.

"You look real nice, son."

"Thanks." He drank from his beer. "Have you been resting like the doctor told you?"

"I've been trying."

"You look tired."

"I know."

"Son-of-a-bitch!" said Craig.

Don looked up. "Told you they weren't gonna make it."

Craig turned with a scowl. "Who the hell's askin' you? Why don't you go and talk somewhere else? I can't hear the damn game."

"Well, don't take it personal."

"How the hell am I supposed to take it?"

"Just forget it, dad."

Sharon tried to change the subject. "How's Stacey?"

"I don't wanna talk about that right now."

"Don't give up on her, son. She's a special lady."

"I said I didn't wanna talk about it."

Craig raised his voice. "You gonna let me listen to the damn game, or what?"

"Let's go to the dining room," Sharon whispered. "Let your dad watch the game."

Don gave her a rebellious look.

She quietly took his hand and pulled him to the dining room table.

"Why do you put up with his crap?" said Don.

Sharon kept hold of Don's hand.

"Don't talk like that about your father."

"Why do you defend him so much? He pushes you around like always. Look at you. He's wearing you out. You're wasting away."

Her eyes turned downcast. "I know I'm not much to look at, son, but talking like that isn't gonna help me or your dad. He needs us—even if he won't admit it."

"What for? So he can push you around?"

"He wasn't always like this, you know."

"You could've fooled me."

"Don," she said tenderly, "I know I've said this before, but I don't wanna leave this world before seeing him make peace with God. You know how embittered he is about his heart condition. I'm the only thing he has to keep him going."

"That's bullcrap."

"No, it's not. He lost you and your brother a long time ago. He was very rough with both of you. That's true. But I think even he realizes that now. What we all need to do is forgive once and for all."

"What are you talking about, mom? Did you hear what was going on in there? I *was* trying. He's the one that refuses."

Sharon took a deep breath and lowered her voice, almost to a whisper. "Don, the reason your dad's sitting out there in the living room watching TV isn't that he's tired of working. The truth is he feels useless. People don't come to him with work anymore. He's too old and sick, and they don't trust his work anymore. His whole life revolved around work. You know that. And even though it didn't seem like it, he tried to make a better life for us."

"Well, I wish he hadn't tried so hard."

"I know. But that's the way things happened, and we need to make things better."

"Sounds like *you* need to talk to him, not me. I don't think he even wants us around. Didn't you hear what he said about Tim?"

"I have talked to him. But he's so angry with himself, he doesn't know how to deal with what he's lost. He's finally realizing that having a house doesn't mean much if you lose everything else. And his pain and anger only keep him repeating the same mistakes. It's an ugly cycle." She took a deep breath. "What he said about Tim was only because he hates what's happening to him. And he thinks Tim's just making excuses."

"That's what I mean."

"They're just words, Don. You need to listen to the pain behind the words. You know how proud he's always been. Always talking about how his kid's gonna do this. His kid's gonna do that. Now he sees what's happening to himself, and on top of that, he sees what's happening to Tim. And now you and Stacey. Don't you see?"

"No, I don't."

"Don, he's sick. What's left of his life is being limited to living it through his kids. And he knows it. The problem is he can't accept it." She let her words resonate. "Don't let the same thing happen to you, son. You need to talk to Stacey. Take her somewhere nice, like you used to. Maybe things can still work out."

"I don't need to talk to *anybody*."

Sharon just looked at him.

"I was so happy when you got married," she pleaded. "I knew she was exactly what you needed. You need to take care of her, son. She'll always love you for that."

"It's too late, mom."

"It's never too late. That's what I'm trying to tell you. If I gave up on your father now, it would undo everything I've tried to do for him."

"Maybe that's what you should do."

"You need her, Don."

"I don't *need* anybody!"

"Don't be like that, son. Don't let your pride get in the way. There's nothing wrong with needing your wife."

"It sounds like you need her more than me. Why don't you talk to her?"

"I have."

Don scowled at her. "What the hell you been talkin' to her about?"

Sharon cowered. "Just to be more patient with you."

"I don't need your help, mom. Why don't you save your sweet talk for someone else and let me work this out myself?"

"I'm just trying to help, son."

"Well, go help someone else. I can take care of my own life."

"Don, please try. She's the best thing you have."

"I know, mom!"

Sharon held her tongue, allowing his words to sink in.

. . . .

Don sat on the living room couch as Sharon came out of the kitchen with a hot plate of nachos. The aroma filled the room as she put the plate on the coffee table, where both Don and Craig could reach it. The television was still on, and UCLA had increased its lead. Craig lay back on his recliner, consoling himself with his beer.

"You want some nachos, dad?" said Don.

"No."

"Come on. They're pretty good."

"I said no!"

Don grabbed his beer and took a long drink.

"Why don't you just relax, dad? You're always so damn tense."

Craig spun around. "Why don't you be quiet and let me watch the game?"

Don turned to Sharon, whose eyes implored him.

"Fine, dad." He leaned back on the couch. "You need help with the yard or something?"

"No. It's fine."

"Is there anything I can help with?"

"What's the matter with you?" Craig sneered. "Don't you have anybody else to talk to? Is that why you came?"

"Cut it out, dad."

"Cut it out? Look at yourself. You ain't no good without that damn woman, are you?" He shook his head. "Is that what I taught you?"

"No, dad."

"Then what the hell's goin' on? I heard they saw 'er with someone yesterday. She's still your wife, isn't she? I don't understand how you can keep this town in order—but not your own wife."

"I'm workin' on it, dad."

"Well it sure don't seem like it."

"It's not that easy."

"The hell it's not. Make her respect you, or find someone who will. You realize what some people are sayin' about you?"

Don's face cringed, and his voice deepened. "What?"

"An' I have ta listen to it. Makes me wanna puke and hide."

"What the hell they saying, dad?"

"Same thing I'm tellin' you. An' those damn rumors you're spreadin' about Stacey—they're makin' you look just as bad as her. Keep your private life to yourself, or people're gonna think you're shit. Didn't I teach you anything?" He mumbled something to himself. "You probably wouldn't even be police chief if it wasn't for me."

"Give me a break, dad. Whatta you want me to do?"

"Aren't you listening? I'm telling you, but maybe you ain't man enough to do it."

"I just came over to talk, dad." Sharon squeezed Don's hand between her own. His throat swelled up as his voice turned high-pitched and submissive. "Why do you always have to make me feel like crap?"

"Don't give me that bullshit." Craig tried to smash an empty beer can between his hands. "You're startin' to sound like you're fifteen again."

"Why can't you give me some credit for once?"

"Credit for what?"

"For at least trying." He quickly wiped his eyes.

"Trying what?"

"Trying to talk to you, dad? You know how long I've been trying to have a normal conversation with you?"

Craig turned back to his television. "I don't have anything else to say. I didn't raise my kids to be a bunch of damn prissies."

Don composed himself and stood up from the couch. "Thanks, dad."

He glanced at his mom and headed out.

She got up and scurried after him as best she could.

"Where the hell you goin', woman?" Craig yelled. "That's why those kids turned out the way they did." He went back to his game. "Damn shit."

. . . .

"Don! Don!" pleaded Sharon after him.

"What?" Don snapped, as he turned to face her. His eyes swollen.

She stopped suddenly. "You know how your father is. I don't want him to get to you like this."

"I'm sick of his crap. He's never satisfied. Even when I became chief—all he could say was that it took me long enough."

"I know, but don't talk about him like he's an ogre."

He stretched out his neck at her. "Well how the hell am I supposed to talk?"

She felt a great weight caving in on her.

"Don't talk like that!" she cried.

Don wavered.

When he took a step toward her, she embraced him firmly.

His hands remained by his side.

"I'm sorry, mom."

"I love you, son."

He hesitated. "I love you too, mom."

"Please promise me you'll keep trying."

Don didn't answer.

She loosened her embrace and looked into his eyes.

Don looked away.

"Why?" he said.

"Don, please." She gasped. "It'll make me happy."

Don nodded.

"You promise?"

"Yeah."

He slowly turned away and strode to his car.

"Thank you for coming, son."

"Bye, mom."

CHAPTER **8**

Don walked up to the second floor of Maplewood apartments, knocked on door number 221, and waited. He still felt like an idiot. How could a grown man be so troubled about having been scolded by his dad? And what was worse—though he didn't want to admit it—he was afraid his dad might be right.

He rolled his head back and took a deep breath. At least the drive through the back roads had helped. He felt somewhat better now. More focused. A bit more relaxed. One way or another, he was gonna fix things. He'd make sure of it.

He looked at his watch, and knocked again.

The door opened slowly.

"What are you doing here?" said Stacey, gazing at his shirt and tie.

He sucked in his gut. "Just wanted to see how you were."

"Really?"

He tried to sound as casual as possible. "Yes, really."

"Is this about last night?"

"No! It's not about last night."

"Are you sure? 'Cause I don't wanna hear it."

"*Yes*, I'm sure." His eyes narrowed slightly. "Can I come in?"

"I suppose."

Don walked into the empty apartment, having second thoughts about making the call. It wasn't like him, and they both knew it.

"You wanna sit down?" Stacey pointed to the pinewood table next to the kitchen.

He took a seat. "Why didn't you bring your stuff?"

She sat down opposite of him. "I didn't wanna create more problems."

"Whatta you mean, 'more problems'?"

"Oh, come on, Don. Don't act like you don't know what's going on."

Damn-it! he thought. There she was again—ruining the mood. And she was so damn good at it. Every time he made an effort, she just had to screw it all up. Wasn't it obvious what he was there for? Isn't that what she wanted? For him to make the first move. She might even be laughing at him on the inside, for all he knew. And she still had the nerve to fuss about it.

He wasn't sure whether to go on or tell her to go to hell.

Next thing he knew, he felt as if his mother reached from behind and tapped him on the shoulder. He turned cold—and almost looked behind—until he realized the absurdity of it.

He composed himself, determined not to let Stacey win so easily.

"You don't wanna move back?" he said.

"No, Don." She gave him a sharp look. "I moved out for a reason."

"Why? You never told me anything. You just got up and left."

"What was I supposed to do? You didn't wanna hear about *my problems*, remember? You had enough of your own to worry about."

"I think I at least deserved an explanation."

"And how would that've helped? Would anything have changed?"

He wasn't sure how to answer.

"Why'd you have to do this to me?" he said, finally.

Stacey shook her head. "Why did I have to do *what* to you?"

"Just leave all of a sudden."

"Don, I tried to live with you for twelve years. There was nothing sudden about it."

"Can't we just talk about it?"

"Talk about what? I tried to talk to you for years, and you wouldn't give me the time of day. All you wanted was for me to smile behind you on your way to becoming police chief. Well, now you're there. And I hope you're happy. I really do. But I have to get on with my own life."

"What about everything we shared together? Doesn't that mean anything to you?"

Stacey responded with a questioning gaze. "I honestly don't know what you're talking about. I've hardly shared a memory with you since we got married. I just happened to be there at the same time—in your way, mostly. At least that's how you made me feel."

Don tried to give her an example. But his mind seemed to clog up.

He cursed himself in silence. That didn't mean the memories didn't exist, for God's sake. He was just frustrated. He couldn't think. Couldn't she see that? Why the hell did she have to push him to the limit all the time? Did he have to get all soppy for her to understand? Hadn't she gotten over that by now?

"I want you to come back with me," he said.

Stacy laughed. She couldn't help herself.

Don's face contorted. "Don't you laugh at me—damn-it!"

"Listen to yourself. You can't even *ask* me to come back with you." Her face saddened. "All you can do is find the energy to *tell* me to come back. I'm sorry, but I can't do that."

"Why?" His brows narrowed. "Are you seeing Qüintero? Is that what this is about?"

"That's none of your business."

"The hell it isn't! Are you seeing him, or not?"

"There's nothing to tell."

"Stop screwing around with me!" He slammed his fist on the table. "Wasn't that son-of-a-bitch gonna be a priest, or something? What the hell's he doin' back, and why are you hangin' around with him?"

"That's none of your business."

Don jumped out of his chair. He pointed a finger at her. "If you wanna play these stupid games, that's fine. But I'm warning you—I'm gonna nail that bastard so bad, you'll wish you'd come back."

"He hasn't done anything!"

He tilted his gaze. "Does breaking someone's nose remind you of anything?"

"That was Mike's fault, and you know it."

"I could care less. Once we get that restraining order, the rest is just a matter of time."

Stacey's eyes teared up with indignation.

"Don't tell me you're gonna cry for that bastard."

"I'm not crying. I'm just imagining what a pleasure it would be to smash your head in right now."

"Oh, really? So you're crying for me?"

She took a deep breath. "I've cried many times because of you." She shook her head. "Never for you. And it appears that I never will."

Don's lips puckered with anger. "I'm telling you. You better cut this shit out right now, or that bastard's going down. And you're going down with him."

"You know what your problem is, Don? You don't know the first thing about love. You're just as oblivious as your dad."

"You leave my dad outta this."

"You think that once you're married your job is over—because the conquest is complete. But love's not a conquest—and it has no end." She paused. "It's a constant nurturing. When you figure that out, the whole world will open up before of you."

"Oh, really. The way it's opened up for you?"

"I never said I was perfect." Her tone saddened. "In fact, the reason we have so many problems in this world is that too many of us have forgotten what love is all about. We think it's about satisfying our feelings—when it's really about sacrificing for one another."

"Cut the crap, Stacey. You're starting to sound like my mom."

"Now there's a smart woman." Stacey's eyes reanimated. "Maybe you should listen to her more often."

Don scowled. "You better stop while you're ahead. And you better stop seeing my mom."

Stacey snickered. "Is there anyone I can talk to without your permission?"

"You know what I'm talking about."

"Your mom needs a friend. And if you're not gonna be there for her, I certainly will."

"You stay out of my family's life, you hear me?"

"I'm sorry." Stacey looked genuinely confused. "I thought you wanted me back."

"You know what I mean."

"You can do whatever you want, but I'm not abandoning your mom. I don't give a damn what you say."

"I'm warning you!"

"Please leave." Stacey pointed to the door. "I don't wanna see your face anymore. You can't hurt me any more than you have already."

"We'll see about that. This doesn't end here!"

"I know, Don. It never ends. That's why I left."

Don beheld Stacey with disgust—before grabbing his chair and hurling it against the wall. He took two steps back, waiting for a reaction. When none came, he turned and charged his way out the front door, making sure to slam it behind him.

CHAPTER 9

After a much-needed workout and shower, Stacey rummaged through the refrigerator, trying to figure out what to cook for dinner. She pulled out some artichokes and poured herself a glass of Chardonnay, wondering if she should make some *albondigas*. It used to be one of Antonio's favorite dishes. His mom had taught her how to cook them, although Stacey never got the opportunity to make them before he left for the military.

The doorbell rang.

She adjusted the flame on the boiling pot of water and went to answer.

As she walked across the living room, the only objects filling the void were a sofa recliner and a small bookshelf teeming with all her favorites—*The Catcher in the Rye*, *The Complete Stories* of Flannery O'Connor, *To the Lighthouse*, *The Stranger*, and the rest of her English major collection of books.

Stacey opened the door. The afternoon had slowly given way to an invasion of clouds that now dominated the sky, although the sun's permeating brightness remained.

"You said you wouldn't be here 'til seven," said Stacey.

"I know," said Antonio. "I couldn't wait. I thought I'd come over so we could go shopping for dinner together."

He had changed into more casual slacks and a shirt.

"I have something cooking already."

"That's okay, just turn it off 'til we come back."

"Why? What's going on?"

"Just trust me."

"O-kay." She kept her eyes on him. "Come on in. Hope you don't mind an empty apartment."

Antonio followed her in, eyeing the bookshelf. "Why should I? I don't have anything to speak of myself."

"I left almost everything at the house. I didn't want any reminders."

"Understandable."

"Actually, I wasn't sure what to make for dinner. I just started cooking some artichokes for an appetizer."

"Don't worry. We'll figure it out," said Antonio. "I would've brought some groceries with me, but I thought it might be more interesting this way."

Stacey smiled. "More interesting?"

"You know that lady John's been thinking about?"

"Maria Lopez?"

"Yeah. You know her?"

"Not really, but I know her son. He's a good student."

"John says he sees her at the grocery store all the time, but he doesn't wanna talk to her. I was hoping we might bump into her?"

"Are you scheming?"

"Yup. I say we make John regret not wanting to join us for dinner."

"Let's do it." She grabbed her purse and car keys with enthusiasm. "I've been waiting for him to do something, but you're right. We're just gonna have to help him a little."

They locked the front door and trotted down the stairway.

"This is what I was thinking," said Antonio. "Since you're the high school principal, and you know—what's the kid's name?"

"Raul," she said.

"Well, since you know him, and you say he's a good student, maybe you can convince his mom to join us for dinner sometime. Tell her you're really impressed with him—which is true—and you and John would like to discuss what you think are serious possibilities for his future. Tell her about scholarships. Whatever you think will help him."

"I can't do that."

"Why not?"

"I'm the high school principal. I can't go around manipulating people like that."

Antonio reflected. "But the bottom line is you'd be doing a good thing, right?"

Stacey did not answer.

Antonio continued, "What if I talk to her myself—and let her know how you guys feel about her son? Would that be okay?"

"I suppose. But what about John?"

"We'll just tell 'm we're going out for dinner. He'll figure things out once we meet up with Maria and Raul."

Stacey stopped by the passenger side of her car. "How do you think he'll react?"

"He'll probably be upset at first, but he'll get over it."

"Deal," said Stacey.

She unlocked Antonio's door and walked around to the driver's side, where Antonio had already unlocked hers from inside.

. . . .

Once they arrived at Don Quick's, the local supermarket, Antonio grabbed a shopping cart and made his way around the cash registers.

"What if we don't see her?" said Stacey.

"Don't worry. John said this was the time she usually comes."

"I'm sure she doesn't shop every day, though."

He smiled. "Then I guess we'll have to come back tomorrow."

He picked up a quart of strawberry yogurt.

"You haven't told me how your first day on the job went," said Stacey.

"Nothing special. But we did go see Anne and the kids for lunch. That was nice. Then Jack insisted we go out for a couple of drinks after we tore down this old shed. I told him I didn't feel up to it. But a lot of good that did."

"How's he doing?"

"Good. But he made me feel guilty as heck for not inviting him last night."

"Did you tell him what happened?"

"He already knew."

"Don?"

"That's what he said."

She shook her head. "I should've known."

"Don't worry," said Antonio. "We can't let 'm get the best of us. That's exactly what he wants. We just need to go about our business."

Stacey grinned. "It doesn't bother you?"

"No, not any more. We can't let other people determine our emotional state of mind."

Stacey hesitated. "He came by today."

"Don?"

"Yeah."

"Wha'd he say?"

"He said he didn't want me seeing you or his mom anymore."

"What happened?"

"Nothing. I just told him to go to hell."

"Why wouldn't he want you seeing his mom?"

"Probably because she's on my side most of the time. For all I know, he might even think we're conspiring against him."

"What happened between the two of you, anyway?"

She fell silent.

"That's okay," said Antonio. "You don't have to say anything."

"Actually, I want to." Her tone lacked conviction. "I don't think he ever really loved me—at least not in the true and enduring sense. And as much as I hate to say it, I think he only wanted to marry me in order to secure a decisive triumph over you."

Antonio frowned. "That's stretching it, don't you think?"

"Then how do you explain that he didn't seem to care about me or the divorce—except for the sake of his career and reputation—until now. Now that you're back, it seems to be very personal again—like when you left for Korea."

She wiped a tear from her eye.

"Maybe it's better not to think about it," said Antonio.

"But it makes so much sense now."

"I just don't want it affecting you like this."

"It wouldn't—if only you didn't have to get caught up in this mess and hear all the vicious rumors he's spreading about me."

He took her by the shoulders. "Don't worry. Those who care know what kind of person you are. That's all that matters." He looked for a spark of hope in her eyes. "We can't control Don, but we *can* forgive him. And we do it for our own sake, remember? To free ourselves of any grief or bitterness."

Stacey returned his gaze. "I miss hearing you talk like that."

Antonio smiled. "Let's keep looking for Maria before we miss her."

As they passed by the juice aisle, he grabbed a half gallon of orange-pineapple. He also took a bundle of bananas.

"You need any tomatoes?" he asked.

"Just a couple," said Stacey.

He put four in a bag and selected a medium-sized cabbage, along with a head of lettuce. "You still like salads, right?"

"Of course."

Stacey sorted through the mushrooms.

"Oh, my God," she said. "There's Raul."

Antonio turned. "Where?"

"Over there, by the bread." She pointed.

"Is that his mom?"

"I guess."

"Wow! John still has good taste."

Maria moved about gracefully with curled tresses swinging at her back. She wore a thin sweater that reached down to her waist and a business skirt that completed the look of a woman who inspires respect.

"Whatta you wanna do?" said Stacey.

"Let's just go over and tell her what we discussed."

"What if she says 'no'?"

"Don't worry. She won't. There's no reason to be nervous. Just tell her what we talked about."

She gave Antonio a blank look. "You said *you* would tell her."

"Okay, we'll both tell her."

"That wasn't the agreement. Besides, what if she doesn't speak English?"

"You can handle it."

Stacey's eyes opened wide.

"Just follow my lead," said Antonio.

"Okay, you first." She moved to the side and motioned him by.

"But you need to introduce me."

"Oh, all right."

Antonio followed with the shopping cart.

"Mrs. Lopez?"

Maria turned. "Yes?"

"Hi, my name is Stacey. I'm the principal of the high school."

"Yes, nice to meet you."

Stacey smiled at the sound of her English.

They shook hands.

"And this is a friend of mine—Antonio Quintero."

"*Mucho gusto, Señora*," said Antonio.

"*El placer es mío.*"

"And how are you, Raul?" said Stacey.

"Good."

"Stacey tells me you have a very intelligent son, *Señora*."

Maria gleamed with pride.

"Why don't you tell her what you were just sharing with me, Stacey?"

Stacey glared at Antonio, biting her tongue and trying to control the sudden panic brought about by his treachery.

She turned to Maria. "I'm . . . uh . . . glad we had the opportunity to bump into you, Mrs. Lopez." She gave Antonio another glance. "Antonio's right. I . . . I've been wanting to congratulate you on having such a wonderful son. He's one of our best students."

"Thank you," said Maria.

Raul blushed.

"I hear nothing but good things about him," Stacey continued. "And I was . . . uh . . . wondering if the two of you might have some time to spare one of these evenings. Perhaps dinner. I'd really love the opportunity to talk to you about the promising future we see ahead of Raul. And I know there's at least one other teacher who would love to join us."

"Thank you," said Maria. "That would be nice."

"Great! When do you think you might have some time?"

"I think maybe the day after tomorrow." Maria turned to Raul. "*Está bien?*"

"*Sí*," said Raul.

"Good. How 'bout if I give you a call to confirm?"

Maria agreed, making sure to give Stacey her phone number.

As they walked away, Maria put her arm around Raul and whispered something into his ear.

"That went well," said Antonio. "You seem to have made their day."

"I cannot *believe* you!"

"What? You did fine."

"I was a nervous wreck." She bounced the palm of her hand on her forehead.

"No. You did fine. I'd never have known."

"Well, I hope we did the right thing."

Antonio winked. "Don't worry. John'll thank us one of these days."

"I hope so. She seems nice."

"She has my approval." He grabbed the shopping cart. "So . . . whatta you want for dinner?"

Stacey thought for a moment. "Why don't we just get a club sandwich and go to the park?"

"Right now?"

"Well, maybe not. It looks like it might rain."

"No, let's do it. Who cares! We'll take our chances."

"Okay."

They paid for the groceries and two club sandwiches, then drove to Bruning Park in the center of town. The overcast sky remained decisively translucent, highlighting the scene with an array of deeper hues that seemed to yield a life of their own. Emerald grass thrived under palm trees that hung like giant chandeliers, while the park square remained surrounded by Rockwellian-style homes. Even St. Joseph's Parish, under the weight of its looming bell tower, appeared more animated in white. In the middle of the park lay the municipal pool, where both Stacey and Antonio had learned to swim when they were young. They sat on the grass, next to the fence enclosing the pool, as a slight breeze brushed through the leaves of the eucalyptus above them.

"Remember that day in swimming lessons," said Stacey, "when everyone was supposed to jump into the deep section of the pool?"

"Yeah," said Antonio, his mouth full of turkey on rye.

"I can't believe you were so chicken. You were the last one to jump in, and it didn't seem like you were gonna do it at all."

Antonio stopped chewing. "I wasn't sure what to expect."

"Neither did I, but I did it anyway."

"What can I say?"

Stacey smiled. "I guess there isn't much to say."

Antonio slowly reached out and touched her cheek.

"You know what I love about your smile?"

"What?"

"It's one of the most sincere smiles I've ever seen."

Stacey blushed.

"What's the matter?" said Antonio.

"Nothing." She glanced up when a raindrop fell on her cheek. "It's starting to sprinkle."

Antonio looked around, feeling a drop on his hand and another on his temple. "My dad used to love the rain." He took a deep and prolonged breath. "I can never forget the smell of it saturating the ground when we lived on the farm." He smiled at the sensation of another droplet on his lips. "It's unforgettable—that earthy, piercing smell. My dad always talked about how great it was. He'd go on and on about how much we needed rain, that there was nothing like it, and how it purified everything around us. Sometimes we'd be fishing in the rain—and as long as it didn't pour too hard, we'd just go on fishing. That's when he opened up the most and I felt closest to him. At first my mom would get frustrated when we came home wet, but she got used to it. She'd just frown and shake her head."

Stacey reached over and softly kissed the side of his lips.

"I love you, Antonio."

He looked at her with penetrating eyes as the drizzle played with her face. A drop caressed its way down her cheek. Another splashed her brow and refreshed her nose. And all the while, her lips radiated with color.

"I love you too, Stacey. But we can't go jumping into things."

"I just wanna take care of you. I don't care about anything else. I wanna make up for all the years I made us lose."

He caressed her cheek. "Things just turned out that way. It wasn't either of our fault."

Stacey threw her arms around him.

He propped himself for balance, hugging her as best he could.

"Everything's gonna be okay," said Antonio.

"I know," she whispered. "You wanna leave before the sandwiches get wet?"

She released him.

"No. Let's stay 'til we finish."

"Okay."

But a sudden apprehension came over Antonio. "On second thought, maybe we *should* leave, before we forget where we are."

"That's probably a good idea."

. . . .

They drove around town, reliving memories of the old sites, until the growing darkness prompted them back to the apartment.

Stacey flipped the light switch as they finished drying their shoes on the doormat.

"Let me take your jacket," she said. "I'll set it in front of the heater so it can dry."

Stacey took off her shoes, expecting Antonio to do the same.

He hesitated.

"Aren't you gonna take off your shoes?"

"No," said Antonio. "I should go."

"You should dry up first. You could get sick."

"I should really get going."

Feeling the weight of his words, she shook off her jacket and withdrew into herself.

"You're regretting our time together, aren't you?"

"We just need to be careful. That's all. We can't afford any regrets."

"Why? I'm not afraid of what might happen. I'm willing to do anything for us. Don't you understand?"

"I do understand. That's why we need to be careful. Besides, I already told you I plan to finish seminary. I can't just turn my back on everything I've committed to for the past eight and a half years."

A frustration welled up in Stacey's eyes. "I guess I can't expect to compete with God, can I?"

"You can't look at it that way." Antonio zipped up his jacket. "When I was in seminary, there wasn't a day I didn't think about you and pray for your happiness."

"Then why do I feel so miserable? Why did God bring you back if we can't be together?"

"I don't know."

He reached out and held her cheeks between the palm of his hands, kissing her temple as affectionately as he could.

Stacey just looked at him.

"I don't understand," she said, no longer holding back the tears.

"I don't always understand myself."

He tried to wipe her tears with the back of his fingers.

She considered dropping the subject, but the words rolled out. "If God takes you away, He's gonna have to help me understand why, because I don't think I can do it again."

Antonio gave her a sympathetic gaze. "Whatever happens, God *will* help us."

He released her with a hurried good night.

Chapter 10

The doorbell rang a few minutes later.

Stacey looked up from the recliner and hesitated. She looked around, wondering what Antonio might've forgotten, but she saw nothing. Feeling a headache coming on, and not wanting to think more than she had to, she forced herself up and answered the door.

Don's hand immediately reached in, taking hold of the door stile.

He looked in with piercing eyes, then pushed his way in.

"Whatta you want, Don?"

"That was a hell of a public display at the park."

"You still have your little spies checking on me? I already told you, it's none of your business."

"The hell it's not! You're still my wife, so you better watch yourself."

"I don't need to watch *anything*. We're practically divorced."

"It's not final."

"I've had enough abuse, Don. This isn't the type of thing you toy around with."

He got in her face. "*I* never cheated on you."

Stacey sighed. "You think I don't know the truth? Just because I never said anything? You weren't even discrete about it."

He took a step back. "We could've talked."

"Didn't we just go through this a few hours ago?"

Don closed the door behind him. "Why are you pulling this shit on me?"

"I'm not pulling anything on you. Whatever I do, I do to myself."

Don refused to take his stare off of her.

"And stop looking at me like that," said Stacey. "You've never given a damn about anyone but yourself."

"I love you, damn-it! What the hell do you want me to say?"

She looked him over, trying to figure out if he was truly making himself vulnerable. She couldn't remember the last time it happened. She actually felt bad for him.

"Nothing," said Stacey. "There's nothing you can do anymore. I told you already."

"I'm here! Just let me make things up."

"I don't need you anymore."

Don's eyes bulged. "And now you're gonna tell me you need that bastard Qüintero, right?"

"As a matter of fact, yes. I do." She snickered. "But don't worry. He doesn't want me. What you would kill to have back, he doesn't even want. Isn't that ironic? And I don't blame him. I let him down when he needed me most. I can't expect him to still want me after mucking up my life with yours."

"You're still my wife, damn-it." He pointed his finger at her. "So don't go around acting like a little whore."

"If you don't want me acting like a whore, then why don't you stop spreading those damn rumors about me?"

Don swung his arm, slamming the wall to his right.

Stacey flinched.

"I'm sorry!" Don clenched his eyes. "Why can't we just try again?"

"I already said 'no'!"

"Why? Why the hell do you have to say 'no'?"

"Because it's too late. That's why."

"What does that bastard Qüintero have to offer you, anyway?"

"Just his time—and his love. Something you were always too busy for."

"I thought you said he didn't want you?"

"He doesn't." She paused for emphasis. "But he does love me, and he's smart enough to know that his manhood isn't threatened because of it."

Don fixed his eyes on her. "You *will* come back to me."

"What're you gonna do? Force me?" She tried to gauge his resolve. "I'd kill myself before letting it happen. I never should've married you in the first place."

His eyes went wild. "You better cut this shit out right now!"

"Or what?"

Don hesitated. "I'll think of something."

Stacey laughed out loud.

The high pitch struck a deep nerve with Don, and before he knew it, his right arm pulled back. With a clenched fist, his arm shot forward and exploded into Stacey's eye socket.

Her body jolted back, and she collapsed limp on her side.

Unaware that she had momentarily blacked out, she tried to prop herself.

"Get out of my apartment!" she said.

Don glared down at her without an ounce of control left. He lunged to the ground with momentum, grasping her by the neck. His other hand reached behind and yanked her hair, jerking her head back. He looked ready to break her cervical. "I swear I'll keep my word and make that son-of-a-bitch regret ever coming back."

Stacey stared—trying to demonstrate control—as her heart raced to get away.

"There's nothing you can do about it," she said.

"Watch me." He leered into her eyes.

"What're you gonna do?" said Stacey. "Beat him up? I don't think you have the guts after what happened to Mike."

Don squeezed her neck harder, bringing his face next to hers. "I'm not going through with this divorce anymore." He gloated. "You can cry, beg, or whatever you want, but you can forget about my signing any more papers. I'll kill you before I let you go back to that bastard."

He pushed her away slowly, and he seemed about to let go, when the grip on her neck tightened once again, depriving her of breath, as he thrust her back against the wall.

Stacey collapsed at the release of his grip, leaving a dent on the sheet-rocked wall.

She looked up through squinted eyes—trying to gather her wits—as she caught glimpses of Don stomping out the door.

"I'm not afraid of you anymore!" she gasped.

She fell over in pain, coughing and holding her side.

CHAPTER 11

For several hours Antonio tossed and turned, trying to get some sleep. Not even a hot shower had helped. He clenched his teeth and pulled the pillow over his head in a losing effort to drown out the racing thoughts. How on earth could he be failing so miserably, even after promising himself that it wouldn't happen?

Stacey deserved better. He couldn't live with hurting her again.

He cried to God for greater strength, but the nagging question of "why" remained.

Why was it turning out so difficult? How, after eight and a half years of discipline, could he still lack the character to do God's will?

He only seemed to be complicating things further.

Definitely not the marks of a good priest.

But torturing himself was not what God wanted either. He sure as heck wouldn't be able to help himself this way—much less somebody else.

He threw off his covers and went into the kitchen, looking for a pencil and paper. As he sat down, John's words resonated in his mind: "Write down everything, Antonio. Everything. There's no better way to understand what's going on inside you. No better way to untangle your thoughts." And over the years he found this to be good advice.

He wrote down all that came to mind. He'd sort it out later, when the words stopped flowing. He wrote quickly, stopping only occasionally to reflect. At one point he closed his eyes, trying to remember Stacey's exact words, before resuming. At least now he was busy and distracted. That in itself brought comfort.

"What the hell," said John. "Don't you ever sleep?"

Antonio looked up to the presence of John in his robe. Then he glanced at the kitchen window, taking note that it was almost morning and starting to rain.

"Whatta you writing? It's gotta be good if you're losing sleep over it."

"Just some thoughts," said Antonio. He thanked God the swelling in John's arm appeared to be subsiding.

"You're losing sleep over some measly thoughts?" John shook his head. "Isn't it time you stop treating me like a stranger? You've hardly been yourself since you got here."

"Whatta you talking about?"

"Come on, Antonio. I know you better than anyone. You've never kept secrets from me. Did something happen with Stacey yesterday?"

"Well—" He winced.

"Whatta you stressing about? I doubt it was that bad."

"No. But it could've been."

John waited for detail that never came. "You mind if I look at what you wrote?"

"Go ahead."

Antonio handed John the sheets of paper, leaving him to read, while he got ready for a jog before Sunday mass.

By the time Antonio returned in full running gear, John was waiting for him.

"It looks to me like you're afraid of putting everything on the line." said John.

"If you're talking about Stacey, I already told you. I can't just turn my back on the priesthood."

"Why not? What if it's the right thing to do? You know better than me that God has an interesting way of timing and working things out."

"It just doesn't make sense to me."

"Why? You don't think she's worth it anymore?"

"I think she's worth more than ever."

"Then I don't understand. If you want to punish yourself, that's one thing. But why punish her? She needs you."

"She's a strong woman. She'll get by without me."

"I agree. But getting by is one thing. What I don't understand is why you wanna deprive her of more."

"I never said I wanna deprive her of anything."

"Okay." He held up Antonio's sheets of paper. "That's what *this* is telling me. But your actions are saying something different. You *want* her to be happy, yet you somehow expect it to happen on its own."

"God does provide," said Antonio.

"Yes, I know. But I'm trying to be practical at the same time."

"You don't think I'm being practical?"

"Sure, in a selfish kind of way."

Antonio's brows narrowed. He wasn't used to being accused of selfishness.

"Whatta you mean, 'selfish'?"

"You're trying to fix a situation without getting involved. Normally, that would be fine, but this time you are involved. And you're trying to fix it from the outside, instead of the inside." He handed Antonio the sheets of paper. "Just look at what you wrote. You can't deny these feelings. Respond to your heart, Antonio, not just your brain. I don't think God would hold that against you."

"It's not that easy—especially if it means turning my back on the priesthood. Can't you understand that? It's part of who I am now."

"Oh, I understand. Believe me. I just can't imagine being able to live with myself, knowing I'm betraying an even bigger part of myself."

Antonio remained silent.

"You wouldn't be the first to have a change of heart concerning the priesthood," John continued. "Did I ever tell you about my great uncle?"

"Not that I remember."

"Well, my mom told me he was gonna be a priest. And about half way through, he met my great aunt. Needless to say, he left the priesthood and they got married. But he never abandoned the church. It remained a significant part of him. He was quite the disciplinarian. I remember my mom saying that, after his sons got married, he occasionally dropped by to visit them. When he didn't find them at home with the family, he went looking for them. And he'd bring them back from wherever he found them—usually the local bar. He didn't beat around the bush. He'd tell them straight out that if they didn't wanna get married, they shouldn't have done so, but since they'd already crossed that bridge, their responsibility was with the family, not the local bar. He kept them in line."

"That's exactly what I've been saying. It's about commitment and responsibility. That's why I can't give up the priesthood."

"Antonio, you're messing up my story. That wasn't the point. The point was that it *is* possible to have a stronger calling than the priesthood, even this late in the process, without betraying the church. Come on, you must realize the potential here. You still love her, so why make things difficult?"

"I don't wanna talk about it anymore. I'm going out for a run. You wanna go to mass afterward?"

"Actually, Stacey and I prefer the afternoon service."

"I'll be right back, then."

He drank a glass of water and headed out the front door.

．　．　．　．　．　．　．　．　．　．　．　．　．　．　．　．

Freshly showered and in his best clothes, Antonio waited his turn at the confessional in St. Joseph's Parish, about half an hour before mass was scheduled to begin. He could still hear the rain outside. He stood in the vestibule, looking at the crucifix against the back wall and the stained-glass window immediately above. The smell of incense and candle wax made him feel at home. Finally, a lady stepped out of the door to his right, and the light above it turned on, indicating the priest was ready to hear another confession.

He walked in and closed the door behind him.

Father Flanagan sat comfortably with another chair next to his. Those who preferred had the option of a kneeler in front of a screened booth.

Antonio opted for the chair.

"Do you remember the Act of Contrition?" said Father Flanagan.

"Yes, Father." Antonio recited the Act of Contrition in its entirety.

"You remember it well." He sounded surprised. "Unfortunately, too many people don't anymore."

"I'm a seminarian, Father."

"Oh, . . ." He looked Antonio over. "How can I help you?"

"I'm in a dilemma, Father." He looked away. "I should probably start by telling you that I left the seminary in Mexico because I was accused of a crime I didn't commit. If I hadn't left, I'd be sitting in jail right now—with little hope of getting out. I couldn't prove my innocence, and there were plenty of people who would've paid to make sure I never got out." He sat up straight. "I came back in hopes of finishing seminary here, but now I've encountered another dilemma. At first I didn't give it much thought, but now it troubles me more than anything. It threatens my commitment to the seminary, and I don't know what to do."

Father Flanagan remained silent.

"Father?" said Antonio.

"Yes, I hear you. What is the nature of this second dilemma?"

"It's a woman, Father."

"I see." An expression of responsibility came over him. "This is a sensitive issue."

"I know, Father. It's been tearing me up inside."

"Do you love this woman?"

Antonio blushed, once again avoiding eye contact.

"Do you love her?" Father Flanagan insisted.

Still, Antonio did not answer.

"Is this Stacey we're talking about?"

Antonio pulled back. "How'd you know?"

"She seems to be on a few people's prayer list lately," he explained.

Antonio remained speechless.

"It shouldn't surprise you," said Father Flanagan. "People love Stacey very much, despite the rumors. And I'm one of them. She's a wonderful person."

"Yes, she is." Antonio looked at him skeptically. "How'd you know it was me?"

"I doubt there'd be two fugitive seminarians roaming around at the same time. I mean that in a neutral way, of course. But you haven't answered my question."

Again, Antonio hesitated.

"You don't necessarily have to answer the question for *me*. But you do have to answer it for yourself. And you have to do so with complete honesty. Lust is one thing, but love is a whole different matter."

"I know, Father."

"It *has* been more than ten years, after all. I would encourage you to keep questioning your motives and take those questions and doubts to the furthest depths of consideration—always asking the deeper questions—just like seminary trained you. This is what it's all about. There's no shame in doing one thing or the other. There's only shame in acting irresponsibly and doing the wrong thing for the wrong reason."

"Yes, Father."

"We were made to love. That was God's whole purpose in creating us. Not necessarily in a romantic sense, but if you must act on your love for Stacey, then do it discretely. Wait until the divorce is final, and make sure it happens before you become a priest. Don't let things get messy. I've seen it happen before, and it's not pretty. The Church suffers a lot as a result of it."

"Yes, Father, I understand."

"Believe me, few things hurt me more than seeing the Church lose a potentially good priest, but if that's the way God has ordained things, who am I to question it?" He thought for a moment. "Don't be afraid, and know that you can count on me for anything. You know you don't need to wait for confession. Just come by, and I'll be here. I know how unjust life can seem at times. We've all had to make our share of decisions. Just make sure your intentions are clean and follow them wholeheartedly."

Antonio gave a slight grin.

"Anything else?" said Father Flanagan.

"Actually, yes, Father. I hurt a young man the other day. I think I broke his nose, and I haven't been at peace about it. It would be easy to say I did it in self-defense, but I didn't need to hit him as hard as I did. The only reason I haven't gone to apologize is that I'm afraid it would make matters worse."

"I can understand the concern. You should try to exercise greater restraint."

Antonio lowered his gaze. "Yes, Father."

"Perhaps a more careful selection of locale would help next time. I understand there's been some brawling issues at the Bighorn lately."

"Yes, Father."

"But that's not something you'd be aware of, having been away for so long." Father Flanagan smiled at this point. "I'll have to talk to John about that one."

The humor eased Antonio's tension.

"For *penance*," Father Flanagan emphasized, "there's just one thing I'd like to ask of you. Assess your heart well! If it's to love Stacey, then do so. It would bring God much joy to see her happy. And if it's not, then I'm sure God has grander things that he's preparing for the two of you."

CHAPTER 12

The rain drummed down as John went to answer the door with his face full of shaving cream. He looked through the peephole, hoping it wasn't anyone important. Stacey expected him to be ready in half an hour.

To his dismay he saw Stacey leaning against the doorway—with head bowed low—hiding behind sagging hair and large-framed sunglasses.

He pulled the door open.

"What's wrong?"

Stacey did not budge or answer.

John wrenched the towel from his shoulder and wiped the remaining soap around his beard, before throwing the dry side over Stacey's head.

"Come in," he said. "You're getting wet. What's wrong?"

"I'm leaving." Her words came out hoarse.

"Huh? Whatta you mean, you're leaving?"

"I can't stay here anymore, John."

"Why? What's going on?" He tried to contain his frustration. "Antonio told me something happened, but I didn't expect anything like this."

"It's not Antonio," she said. "Don came by last night."

John glowered. "What the hell for?"

"Someone must've seen Antonio and me together at the park last evening. Don told me he wasn't going through with the divorce anymore. And he's threatening to make Antonio regret ever coming back."

John took her by the arm and walked her to the living room.

When she pulled the towel down to her shoulders, John caught sight of the purple outline around her eye—and a rancorous rush of blood stormed his face.

"What the hell happened?"

"I guess I really pissed him off this time."

"What happened?"

"I laughed at his threats."

"We've gotta do something. We can't let him get away with this crap. What kind of law enforcement is he, anyway?"

"No! It'll just make things more difficult for Antonio. I already thought about it. It's better if I leave."

"Sit down," said John. "You can't leave. We can't go on as if nothing happened. You have to report this. And even if no one believes it, at least you'll be able to start building a case against him?"

Stacey sat next to him on the couch. "To be honest, I don't think he'll do anything like this again, but I am afraid of what he might do to Antonio."

"So . . . what are you planning to do?"

"Resign as principal and move to Sacramento as soon as possible. Hopefully, my being out of town'll be enough to make Don forget a few things."

"What if he doesn't?"

"Oh, I think he will. As long as he stops feeling an immediate threat to his ego, I don't think he'll even notice."

"What about Antonio?"

She lowered her gaze. "He's got other things he needs to do."

"Don't tell me he's convinced you of that?"

"What am I supposed to think?"

"You *must* know that he still loves you."

"Yes, but he loves someone else even more. I can't compete with that. I don't want to compete with that."

"He'll come around. I'm sure of it."

John stood up and went looking for the sheets of paper Antonio had written earlier.

"Look at what I found him writing this morning," he said.

He tried to hand her the sheets.

She raised her hand in protest.

"No, John. I don't wanna look at anything."

"Give him a chance. Don't just give up on him again." He caught himself. "I'm sorry. That's not what I meant."

Stacey winced. "No, you're right. I deserve it. I'm being just as fickle as last time."

"Just give him a chance. That's all I'm saying. I think we need to understand that, in his mind, his entire life was already mapped out. He'd already given up on a wife and family. I imagine it's like seeing a loved one come back from the dead."

She considered his words with a deep sigh.

"I have to admit," she conceded, "we think we're so prepared for anything—that we've learned so much from life. But when the moment of truth arrives, all those notions of a strong, assured self are so easily shattered. At least Antonio admits his weakness when he sees it."

John remained silent.

"What I should've done," said Stacey, "was move to Sacramento in the first place. I could've commuted and avoided all this mess."

"There you go!" said John. "Why don't you just do that, instead of quitting so abruptly? After all, it wouldn't look good for your superintendent position."

"I don't really care anymore."

"You have to care. I care. I'm not gonna let you throw everything away."

Stacey closed her eyes and wrapped her fingers around her forehead.

"God!" she said.

"What?"

"Why do you have to make things so difficult? I'd already made my decision."

"Because I care."

She shifted over on the couch and threw her arms around him.

"I love you so much, John. I really don't know what I'd do without you."

"I love you too, Stacey. But there's someone who loves you more."

"You are such a conspirator." She hugged him long and hard. "Don't you ever give up?"

"Not if I care enough."

She released him with a smile and tears in her eyes.

"You think you can help me move to Sacramento this week? I can start looking for a place today."

"Just like that?"

"Why not? I'll just take the first decent place I find."

"Sure," he said. "But with one condition."

"What's that?"

"You can't lose hope."

"No, John." She conceded a smile. "With you by my side I could never lose hope."

He returned the smile. "That's my girl."

CHAPTER 13

In lighter spirits Antonio strolled down Hamilton Street, on his way back to John's house. The rain had paused, but the street still lustered with moisture and a few scattered puddles. It filled him with joy to see the psychology of confession at work in him. Verbalizing his painful memories with another person had helped to clarify and soothe his anguish. But it saddened him to realize how so many refused to confess because they no longer understood the benefit of opening their hearts in front of another mere-fleshed person like themselves.

He appreciated the way Father Flanagan made him feel comfortable. It reminded him of *Padre* Martínez, from his first year in seminary, who had the gift of saying just the right thing to anyone going through difficult times. As it turned out, when some of the seminarians arrived, they spent much of their time trying to validate their calling in the midst of emerging doubt, and it was up to *Padre* Martínez to help them sort things out and advise them accordingly.

His seminary friend, Pedro Mendoza, was a different character altogether. Instead of preoccupying himself with reasons to stay in seminary, he actually looked for reasons to leave. He truly had the calling, *Padre* Martínez had remarked more than once. And every time Pedro wanted to leave, it was *Padre* Martínez who reminded him of the gifts God had given him and what a mistake it would be to take them for granted. Antonio felt fortunate for all the love and grace he'd seen at work through Pedro's struggle. In fact, Antonio might not have lasted as long as he did if it weren't for all he'd seen revealed through their friendship.

He began to whistle a tune before realizing that his father used to sing it to him and his brother when they were young. A smile took over his face.

When he arrived at the house, he found John watching television.

"How was church?"

"Couldn't have been better."

"Really? Maybe I should've gone with you."

"That Father Flanagan's a good priest."

"Yes, he is. He really helped me deal with things after Beth passed away."

"You pretty close with him?"

"Somewhat."

"Have you been talking to him about Stacey and me?"

John did not respond.

"Do I sense a little guilt?" Antonio held back a chuckle.

"Okay. Yes, I did. What's so wrong with that?"

"Nothing. I was just curious." He smiled this time. "You know what I was thinking?"

"What?"

"Seminary's quite an experience. It's as intense as anything I've ever done."

"What's so revealing about that?"

"I don't know. I was just thinking about it."

"What about Special Forces?"

"Well, it's interesting that you ask. I was thinking how both taught me a lot about survival." He rubbed his chin. "I think the most significant thing I learned was how to overcome my own personal barriers for the sake of others. I mean, both experiences took me out of my comfort zone. I did things I never thought myself capable of. The basic difference is that I did one for love of God and the other for love of country. They both showed me that no one is dispensable. And there's *always* a greater purpose. What I *didn't* like about the Army is that they expected us to blindly follow orders. There's a reason for it, of course, but sometimes it felt like too much. In seminary they taught us to constantly challenge ourselves and our views."

"And?" said John.

Antonio took a seat. "Well, when I was in seminary, I was constantly tormented with the thought of Stacey being married. It took me a couple of years to get over it. But . . . you know how I finally came to terms with it?" John shrugged his shoulders. "I convinced myself that I loved her more as a sister than anything else. I mean, I couldn't be in love with a married woman, right? So I convinced myself that I actually loved her as my own sister."

"Are you trying to tell me something, or what?"

"I don't regret any of it. I can even say with confidence that it was the right thing. I don't know where I'd be right now if it hadn't been for my seminary experience."

"Stacey's leaving." said John.

Antonio's mood shattered. "What're you talking about?"

"Just what I said. She's moving to Sacramento."

"Why? Because of me?"

"No, because of Don. He beat her up last night."

"What?" Antonio sprung to his feet. "Where is she? I've gotta see her."

"No!"

Antonio gave him a blank look. "Whatta you mean, 'no'?"

"You just can't see her for the moment. That's all. He smacked her one in the eye."

"Why the heck can't I see her?"

"Because Don made some threats—if he ever saw the two of you together again. She's looking for an apartment in Sacramento right now."

"So . . . what's gonna happen?"

"She figures everything should be fine, as long as you both stay out of sight."

Antonio frowned at the idea. "What are we supposed to do—hide?"

"Of course not. Just make sure you don't bump into Don. And make sure no one sees you alone with Stacey. She's going to the Sheriff's department to file a complaint. She doesn't want to press charges to avoid taunting him further, but she wants there to be a record of what happened—just in case he's serious about not going through with the divorce anymore."

"We can't just let him control people's lives like that."

"I know—and I can understand the frustration—but don't do anything stupid."

"Oh, don't worry. I know better than that." His eyes quivered with thought.

"What's on your mind?"

"Nothing," said Antonio, feeling awkward about changing the subject. "Actually, I'm wondering if Stacey mentioned anything about dinner tomorrow?"

"What the heck does that have to do with anything? This is a serious matter we're talking about here."

"I know. I was just wondering."

"No, she didn't. Why?"

"We're supposed to have dinner with Maria Lopez tomorrow."

John narrowed his glare. "What are you talking about?"

Antonio half-smiled. "You never told me what an attractive woman she is."

"What's that supposed to mean?"

"We kind of bumped into her at the store yesterday."

"Kind of?"

"Stacey and I were shopping for dinner, and we bumped into her, so . . . we invited her to join us for dinner tomorrow night."

John scowled. "What the hell for? Are you listening to what I'm saying?"

"Don't worry. We'll all be together. I won't be alone with Stacey. Besides, we could go to Sacramento. Nobody would see us there. What's the big deal?"

John looked around and huffed. "Wha'd you invite her for, anyway?"

"We just started talking. She seemed like a nice lady."

"Hell! At least you decided to tell me before we showed up."

"Anything to please," said Antonio.

"Look," said John, "I'm gonna please you one on the head if you don't listen to what I'm saying and start taking this seriously."

"Don't worry. I heard you. And I *am* taking you seriously, but I'm not gonna sit around like a dead duck."

John nodded. "Well, you better be careful. And don't do anything stupid."

"Don't worry. I have no reason to."

CHAPTER 14

The red and purple hue of dusk stretched dark shadows over most of Main Street as Don parked his squad car in front of The Flamingo Bar and Grill. After assessing things one last time, he went in, looking for his nephew, Mike. When he did not find him, he crossed the street to Foster's Bighorn, where he found Mike perched at the front end of the bar, smoking a cigarette. Hanging over his head, the taxidermic tigers seemed to growl in protest, as they desperately needed a cleansing from the soot that now covered their formerly bright-orange coats. The trophies hung as a waning testament to Rio Vista's glory days—when the city was self-sufficient and left wanting almost nothing that it could not provide for itself—days of small-town movie theaters; A&W restaurants; and small, downtown businesses that worked together as a family, supporting one another and thriving amidst themselves.

All this, of course, began to erode when large corporations introduced malls and superstores that drove many of them out of business, breaking down their family structure and making the survivors alter their methods for the sake of competition and survival.

"Hey, Mike," said Don. "Your dad told me I'd find you here."

Mike turned. A white bandage covered his nose, with a purple bruise encircling the perimeter. He blended in with his civilian clothes this time.

As soon as he saw Don, he gave him his back.

"Whatta you want, Don?"

"I need to talk to you."

"What about?"

"Can we talk outside?"

"No."

"This is serious, Mike. I think you'll be interested."

Mike turned slowly. "What makes you so sure?"

Don came up close and whispered. "How would you like to nail the son-of-a-bitch that broke your nose?"

Mike looked up with a spark in his eyes. "Okay, I'll hear you out. But it better be good." He turned to the bartender. "I'll be right back, Doug."

He slipped on his jacket as they strolled outside. The evening had cooled too quickly for Mike's taste, and the fog appeared to be coming in.

When Don began to cross the street, Mike stopped.

"Are you coming, or not?" said Don.

"I ain't goin' in that car."

"Don't screw around with me, Mike. I told you—this is serious."

"Well, I ain't goin' in that car."

"Cut the crap, and come over here. I have nothing against you right now. Our business from the other day's been settled. What I have here is a serious proposition. Something we can both benefit from."

Still, he didn't budge.

"Damn-it, Mike!" Don reached out to him. "Here—take the keys. I just wanna talk to you in private."

Mike tentatively accepted the keys, before walking to the car.

Once inside, Don closed his window and turned to Mike.

"Antonio beat up Stacey last night," he said.

Mike looked at him coldly. "What's that gotta do with me? She probably deserved it, for all I care."

Don brushed a hand against his thigh. "You're probably right, Mike, but we still need to do something. This guy's a serious problem."

"You mean *you* have to do something. You're the police chief, not me."

"I thought you wanted to nail this bastard."

"And I thought you didn't give a damn about Stacey." Mike glared with defiance. "You wouldn't even help me the other night. And now that Stacey's involved, you want me to stick my neck out to do your dirty work? Forget it!"

"Damn-it, Mike, we're in this together. We both want the same thing. I just can't do it by myself."

Mike eyes roamed, giving the matter some thought. "What'd you have in mind?"

"I'm gonna keep an eye on him and see what he's up to. Once I figure it out, I'll come and get you. We'll make the son-of-a-bitch regret the day he was born."

"Then you're in on it too, right? It's not just me."

"That's right."

Mike searched Don's face.

Once satisfied, he stretched out his hand. "Okay. Deal."

CHAPTER 15

Antonio arrived at work the next morning, but only after struggling through the thick fog and almost missing his turnoff. When he parked, he noticed Max roaming around the remains of the demolished shack, as if in despair over the loss of a familiar, even if less than desirable, way of life. Antonio thought of Jack's son as he contemplated the bull's musings, and he promised himself to finish the framing for the foundation as soon as possible. Maybe they could even pour the cement in a day or two.

He checked the level in Max's self-feeding barrel, before cleaning out the water trough. Then he strolled behind the tractor shop and returned with half a bale of alfalfa.

"There you go, Max. That should keep you busy for a while."

He made his way to the tractor shop, where Jack was already waiting.

"You're here early," said Antonio.

Jack's stare made him feel self-conscious.

"Ya gotta be straight with me," said Jack. "No more screwin' around. I been hearin' too many things."

Antonio scowled. "About what?"

"I heard ya beat up Stacey yesterday."

"What?" Antonio threw his arms out in protest. "I can't believe this." He shook his head. "I'm trying really hard not to hate Don for all the crap he's pulling, but things just keep going from bad to worse."

"I'll believe whatever ya say, Antonio. But I need ta know."

"Why on earth would *I* hurt her?"

Jack looked relieved. "Was it Don?"

Antonio nodded. "In fact, Stacey's leaving town. I guess she couldn't take any more herself. And I don't blame her."

"So what happened?"

"He took a swing at her." His voice trailed off, "Because someone saw us kissing at the park."

"*Kissin'?*" Jack's eyes opened wide. "So it *is* true."

"What's true?"

"That you and Stacey are together again."

"It—" He felt a rush of blood to his face. "It was barely a kiss. Nothing happened."

"Yeah, right." Jack could no longer hide his excitement. "I knew ya'd come around."

"It's not what you think."

Jack was so giddy he could hardly contain himself. "Come on, Antonio. If ya can't trust me, then who can ya trust?"

"Not many people right now, Jack." Antonio remained somber.

"Oh, come on. I'm sorry I doubted ya. But ya have ta understand—I'm even hearin' this from people I trust." He put a hand on Antonio's shoulder. "If ya ask me, you should *both* get outta here as soon as ya can. But ya've gotta go far enough that Don won't find ya. Just leave him ta moan and groan ta himself. Trust me, that'd be the sweetest revenge."

"I don't know, Jack. John doesn't think Stacey should risk her career like that. He thinks she should wait until school's out or she can find a replacement."

"Screw that, Antonio. I'm tellin' ya—it ain't worth it."

Antonio shook his head in frustration. "No. I'm not gonna run."

"Whatta ya talkin' about? Be reasonable. Nobody's runnin' ya out. In fact, that's probably the last thing Don would want. He can't make your life miserable if ya're not here. Whatta ya gain by stayin', anyway?"

Antonio reflected, giving the matter further thought.

"Maybe you're right," he said.

"Of course, I'm right."

"I'll have to talk to Stacey about it tonight."

"Tonight? Why ya have to wait 'til tonight?"

"Well . . . we're trying to set up John with this lady. We're supposed to have dinner with them." Antonio caught himself. "*In Sacramento*," he emphasized, "so Don won't find out and make a big stink about Stacey and me seeing each other."

"I'm tellin' ya, Antonio. Ya gotta get outta here. This place is no good for you guys."

"Don't worry. I'm thinking about it."

"Ya better."

"What about you? Who's gonna help with the farm if I leave?"

"Hell, who cares. I'll survive."

"What about the shed? We already tore it down, and I don't wanna disappoint your son. Did you have any big plans for today?"

Jack looked out into the fields. "It's pretty foggy out there. We probably won't be able ta get much done 'til this afternoon anyway. Last thing we need is ta drive that tractor into a ditch or somethin'." He made a head motion to where the shed used to be. "We can work on that for a while? I don't wancha havin' any more excuses for not leavin'."

Antonio looked at Jack with hurt feelings. "Come on, Jack. Don't make me feel like I don't know what I'm doing. I might not be handling things perfectly, but I'm doing my best."

"I know," said Jack, almost apologetically. "Anne told me not ta be so nosy, but I'm just tryin' ta help."

Antonio nodded. "I understand."

Jack tapped Antonio with his fist. "Tell me more 'bout John and that lady."

"Oh, you should meet her." Antonio reanimated. "She's pleasant, attractive, and she has the most dazzling hair."

"Sounds too good ta be true."

"She's been on his mind for a while."

"Really? What's takin' him so long?"

"He took Beth's passing pretty hard. I think he's just getting over it."

"That's true," Jack acknowledged. "Anyway, hope ya all have a good time tonight. Just make sure you consider what I told you."

"Don't worry. I know what's at stake."

"Good. Then let's get ta work on that shed. I don't want it hauntin' after us."

CHAPTER 16

A light sprinkle cleared up the remaining traces of fog by the time Antonio and John headed north on Interstate Five to meet up with Stacey and Maria for an elegant dinner at *Il Fornaio* Restaurant. Stacey had agreed to pick up Maria and Raul.

"Come on," said Antonio. "You've gotta be on your best behavior tonight. There's no point in being upset anymore."

"Well, next time you and Stacey make plans for me, I don't wanna be the last one to find out."

"Okay," said Antonio. "I promise."

John glared at the road ahead of him, clearly unsatisfied.

"You know," said Antonio. "I'm starting to think you're just nervous."

"Nervous? About what?"

"How long has it been since you've been on a date?"

"Well, let me see. With a chaperone . . . that would be about forty years."

Antonio snickered. "Come on, John. You know there was no way around it this time. Believe me, we're not here by choice. But that's why you need to be on your best behavior. You know how you can come across sometimes—at least to those who don't already know you. They'll eventually realize you're a heck of a guy, but you don't wanna risk that here."

"Oh, so now you're my love coach as well."

Antonio laughed. "Forget it, John. We'll just have to trust you."

"What makes you think this is what I wanted, anyway?"

"Well, for one thing, you haven't flat out rejected the idea."

John reflected for a moment. "Oh."

. . . .

Antonio and John arrived to a full house at *Il Fornaio* Restaurant. Fortunately, they'd made reservations. The hostess told them Stacey and Maria had not yet arrived and proceeded to walk them, past the boisterous banqueters at the marble-topped bar, to their table.

They sat down to small talk, until their waiter arrived.

"I'll have a beer," said John.

"Wait a second," said Antonio. "Remember what we talked about?"

John gave him a blank look.

"You can't freak her out so soon, John."

"Whatta you talking about? I'm just asking for a beer."

Antonio turned to the waiter. "We'll have two waters for now. We need to talk this over a bit."

The waiter nodded. "I'll come back when you're ready."

"What's the deal?" said John. "I can't even have a beer now?"

"I just don't want you to be tipsy when Maria arrives."

"Who's talking about getting tipsy? I just asked for one beer. If you don't cut the crap, I'm not going through with this anymore."

"Oh, all right," said Antonio. "Maybe it'll relax you a bit."

"If you ask me, you're the one who needs relaxing."

Antonio reluctantly acknowledged. "Maybe I should have a drink myself."

John laughed out loud.

"What?" said Antonio.

"You're a darned enigma. That's what."

Antonio looked at him matter-of-factly. "We're all enigmas. Every single one of us. That's what makes us so interesting and unique—for better or worse."

"Whatever!" said John, and he rolled his eyes. "Let's order those beers. I'm starting to worry about you. You're even losing your sense of humor. I can't remember the last time someone worried so much for me."

. . . .

Antonio and John were so caught up in conversation that they did not notice until Stacey, Maria, and Raul stood next to their table. When Antonio looked up, he was caught off guard by the large patch over Stacey's eye.

Self-conscious, she tried to look away.

Antonio followed her gaze, throwing her a tender smile that he hoped would console her.

She responded with a grin.

John jumped to his feet. "How do you do, Mrs. Lopez?"

"Please, call me Maria."

"Sure thing, Maria." They shook hands. "It's a pleasure to meet you."

He turned to Raul. "And how are you, Raul?"

They all greeted one another and sat down.

By the time they ordered their meals and settled into conversation, Antonio could sense Maria's intrigue over their openness and unique manner of affection.

Raul, although shy, never lost track of the conversation.

Antonio directed himself to Maria. "Like we were saying the other day," He glanced over at John. "John here is one of the teachers who most regards Raul's abilities and potential."

John winced at being spotlighted.

"Isn't that right, John?"

"Uh . . . yes." He turned to Maria. "In fact—uh—I was a little upset at myself for not thinking of this earlier, but we should've made a special effort to invite you to an informational seminar that we have for seniors every year. We talk about the college application process, financial aid, and all kinds of helpful information. You and Raul could've had a head start on the whole process. It's not limited to just seniors."

"Yes," said Maria, glancing over at Raul. "That would've been nice."

Antonio and Stacey gave John a questioning glare.

"I'll tell you what," said John, "since it was really my fault, I could take the time to share that information with you whenever you have some time."

"Thank you," said Maria with a smile. "We'd be extremely grateful."

Her words came out in such a sincere manner that it provoked a vaguely familiar sensation in John. It seemed almost random, and of no consequence—until a certain pull drew him to her eyes. They locked gazes. When his heart began to thump, it was too late. His chest burst with a surge of warmth that provoked his body to a nervous sweat.

"It's always an honor to have a small part in the success of someone who shows so much promise," he said.

Maria blushed, finding it hard to direct her eyes in any particular direction.

Stacey, understanding the gravity of the situation, broke in with a roughing of the throat. "Yes," she said, turning to Raul, "we're all very much impressed with you. I'm curious—how much thought have you given to your future?"

"A lot," said Raul. "My mom and I talk about it all the time."

"Really?" She nodded with approval. "That's nice to hear. Not very many kids have that type of communication with their parents nowadays. In fact, neither do many adults. You should consider yourself very fortunate."

"I do," said Raul.

Maria smiled, overwhelmed by all the attention.

"And what are your plans for college?" Stacey continued.

Raul gave her a big smile. "I want to be an architect."

"Great! That's an excellent career. Anything specific you'd like to design?"

"A house for my mom," he said matter-of-factly.

At a loss for words, they all beamed at Raul.

. . . .

When Antonio looked up from his meal, he noticed every table caught up in their own little world. Not much different from their own. Waiters dashed back and forth, trying to keep up with demand, while a busboy cleaned an adjacent table. For the first time Antonio took conscious note of the high ceiling and windows, the high arches, and the varnished cherrywood pillars surrounding them. He found it interesting how architectural design could contribute such a sense of peace—even amidst the bustle.

Stacey, looking more at ease herself, waved her fork in front of her, trying to swallow, in an effort to say something to Maria.

"You know," she said, "it must've been hard raising Raul by yourself."

"Yes," said Maria, "but my in-laws have always lived close by. They've helped me a lot, especially since my husband died."

"Well, I want you to know that you can always count on me for anything." She rubbed an itch around her eye patch. "In fact, I believe I can speak for all of us."

Antonio and John nodded in agreement.

"Thank you," said Maria. "That means a lot."

Stacey turned to Raul. "And I bet it was especially tough on you, growing up without your father."

Maria tried to say something, but Raul cut her off.

"I was only eight when he died, but my mom tells me about him all the time."

"I bet he was a great guy. After all, he married your mom, right?"

"Yeah." He smiled at his mom. "My grandparents also tell me lots of stories." He proceeded to share. "This one time I was really sick with whooping cough in Mexico, and they were afraid I might die, so they—"

Maria put a hand on his shoulder. "They might not be interested, Raul. Those kind of stories usually bore people who aren't part of the family."

"No, not at all," said Antonio. "I love those stories. They're what keep us rooted and appreciative of our family history."

That was all the encouragement Raul needed. "My grandparent's ranch is about three hours from the main road, and there were no hospitals nearby. They found me some medicines and injections, but I still wasn't getting any better. That's when my grandpa said that donkey's milk was supposed to be good for whooping cough, and they went searching the nearby ranches for a mother donkey. They finally found one they could rent, and not long after I started taking the donkey's milk, I began to get better."

Stacey and John turned to Maria, as if seeking confirmation.

Antonio beheld Raul with full acceptance. "Family history is so important," he affirmed. "It helps us understand and gives direction to our sense of purpose." He looked around the table. "It's kind of like our American barn-raising tradition, which kept our communities together for so long. That sense of knowing each other and working together is so important. Nowadays, it just seems to be every man for himself." He turned to Maria. "I think it's a wonderful thing—what you've done with Raul. It obviously gives him a great sense of identity and motivation. I wish more people would do the same. This world would be all the better for it."

"Well," said Stacey, "with such a loving and stable family, I can see why Raul shows no signs of emotional hang-ups."

Antonio smiled. "That's another way of putting it, but that's part of what I was trying to say."

"Ah-huh." She returned the smile. "Sure it was."

John laughed, while Maria and Raul tried to figure out what was going on.

"I'm sorry, Maria," said Stacey. "You just have to get used to us. At least I hope you can. We're really not as strange as we seem."

"Oh, that's not what I was thinking at all," said Maria.

The waiter stopped by their table. "And how's everything here?"

"Great! Thank you."

"Anything else I can get for you?"

"Not right now. Thanks."

He hastened away.

"You know," said Antonio, toasting with a glass of water, "it's a true blessing to be gathered with all of you tonight. I want you to know what a special moment this is for me, and I want to thank God and all of you for making it possible."

They all picked up their waters and cheered.

"So, Raul," Antonio continued, "I understand that you're a good student and everything, but is there any particular class you might be having problems with this year?"

"No."

"Hmmm. Not even a little?"

"Well, maybe Math."

Antonio grinned, looking over at John. "I thought you were gonna say English for a second."

"Not at all," said John. "He's doing quite well in my class."

"I'm glad to hear that," said Antonio. "'Cause I had a heck of a time in his class."

"He was *your* teacher?" said Raul.

"Oh, yeah. He's much older than he looks."

John gave him a serious glare.

"Actually," said Antonio, "he was still in his thirties when I had him. Best teacher I ever had, too."

"He's just joking about having a hard time in my class, though."

"Actually, no," said Antonio. "I did have a hard time. I just worked extra hard."

"Really?" John straightened up, projecting a deep sense of satisfaction. "I never knew that."

"Well, now you know."

John continued to beam.

"About your math class," said Antonio, redirecting himself to Raul, "I don't know if you're interested, since you are doing well, but I'd be happy to help you in any way I can."

Raul beheld him in silence.

"I don't know how long I'll be around, but I can try and tutor you a little if you want."

Raul remained silent.

"*No seas malagradecido,*" said Maria at his lack of response.

"Oh, no," said Antonio. "He's not being ungrateful. I'm the one who's imposing. I just thought a little extra help might come in handy, but I don't want him to feel pressured about it."

"It's not that," said Raul. "It's just that I've never had a tutor."

"Well, let's not worry about that right now. Just think about it. I'm sure I'll see you again soon."

"Okay."

. . . .

They all stood up, brimming with satisfaction and looking forward to the next opportunity to come together. As they squeezed their way past the busy, marble-topped bar, they put on their jacket and walked out to the elevator lounge.

When John noticed Antonio pulling Stacey to the side, he wanted to protest. They had no right to keep conspiring against him like this, especially if they wanted good things to come out of a promising evening.

He wasn't ready to be left alone with Maria.

He walked over to the elevator, with her and Raul, trying to make it clear that they were waiting and ready to go.

Maria did not seem to mind.

She hugged Raul from behind and smiled. "We had a wonderful time."

John stumbled to respond. "Well . . . thank you for joining us. I'll give you a call tomorrow . . . to remind you that I'm coming by with that information."

"Oh, there's no need to call. I won't forget."

Silence ensued.

John looked over to Stacey and Antonio, hoping they would cut their conversation short. That's when he realized there had been no covert intentions. They simply drifted off spontaneously into a brief and private conversation, which even Maria seemed to appreciate.

. . . .

Stacey noticed Antonio pulling out a sheet of paper from his pocket.

"What's that?" she said.

"It's something I wrote. I wanted to give it to you."

Instantly, she visualized herself in high school chemistry class, with Antonio sitting behind her. It was there that he shared the bulk of his rustic verses. The only problem was that he had written most of them in Spanish when she could still barely read it. But he was so excited to share—and he insisted so adorably that she read them—that she always found it hard to refuse.

Now she felt him doing it again, but this time it was she who couldn't wait to read it.

"It's not in Spanish, is it?"

Antonio chuckled. "No, this one came to me in English."

He handed it to her.

She unfolded the paper with care and read out loud for him to hear:

"My childhood dream was You. My dream is still
You. My only hope is You. You bring
Me back to life when I feel dead
And give me all the love that I once missed.
'I want to take care of you,' you said.
How could I forget? It's made the difference
Since. I never want to go back again.
I'll stay here with you, and take care of you."

Stacey reread the poem in silence before looking up at Antonio's awaiting gaze.

"Does this mean . . . ." She could not get the words past the lump forming in her throat.

"Yes," said Antonio.

"It's very sweet," she managed to say, "but the tone is so sad."

"Maybe that's because it was so hard to reach that conclusion."

She threw her arms around Antonio.

. . . .

At a distance, John tried to absorb the scene without falling victim to emotion. He finally looked away to avoid the temptation.

"I've been waiting for this for a *long* time," he said, controlling his euphoria.

Maria's smile returned a glitter of understanding.

"I wish we could leave them to themselves," John continued, "but Stacey needs to give me a ride home. Antonio needs my car to go see his brother."

"I understand."

"He actually wanted to go back to work, but with all this rain, I talked him out of it."

"Work?" said Maria. "This late?"

"I don't really know. He said he needed to redo some foundation frame."

Maria looked at him like he was crazy.

"I know, but once he gets an idea into his head, there's no stopping him. He said he thought of a better design on the way up here."

"Well, he might be a little strange, but he seems like a sweet person."

"Yes. That he is."

CHAPTER 17

Antonio drove to Rubén's house with butterflies in his stomach, as if returning from prom night. He even took a whiff of his jacket sleeve—to see if he could detect a lingering scent of his embrace with Stacey—and he was not disappointed.

Delighted to see his brother's porch light still on, he went ahead and parked.

He glided all the way to the front door and knocked, excited to share the latest news.

Rubén answered with bloodshot eyes, wearing sweatpants and thermals. The sight of Antonio roused him to straighten up and fling the door open.

"*Pásale!*" said Rubén.

"*Espero que no te haya despertado.*"

"*Por supuesto que no.* I was up with the kids, so now I'm just catching up on some work."

Rubén greeted him with a firm embrace.

"Is everyone asleep?"

"Don't worry. They're deep sleepers."

They walked into Rubén's den and took a seat at the drafting table.

"I remembered you were back from your trip," said Antonio, "so I figured I'd drop by and let you know how things were going."

"Is everything okay?"

"I just came from having dinner with John and Stacey."

"Really? How's the old guy doing?"

"You should give him a call. He's feeling sentimental about not hearing from you."

"Yeah," said Rubén. He shoved some schematics to the side. "I'll give him a call tomorrow. How's Stacey?"

"That's what I wanted to talk to you about."

Rubén leaned forward.

"It's also about Don," said Antonio. "You know how being around him always gets complicated, especially when Stacey's involved."

Rubén gave him one of his elevated-brow, spit-it-out looks.

"Yeah, yeah," Antonio admitted, with a wave of the hand. "It happened. Just like everyone thought."

Rubén grew a smile. "So what now?"

"Well, he made some threats."

"Don?"

"Who else?"

"What kind of threats?"

"Enough to make Stacey wanna quit her job and risk her career."

Rubén waited for more.

"John convinced her to stay for a while—maybe 'til the end of the year. She's trying to find an apartment in Sacramento right now, but I'm thinking it'd be better if I left instead. If anything, it would make Don less suspicious. That's why I was hoping I could come back and stay with you for a while. Maybe not seeing me around would calm things down."

"Of course," said Rubén. "The last thing you need is more trouble."

"I think Jack's right—the further away we go, the better."

"Is that what he said?"

"He's convinced."

"What about you?"

"Well, I hate to run out like that. But . . . if we're gonna do things right, I think we need to disappear after the divorce is final. Otherwise, we're just inviting more trouble."

Rubén kept his eyes on him. "Is there something else?"

Antonio hesitated. "That means we're not coming back."

"It's that bad?"

"Don gave Stacey a black eye the other day."

"What the hell!"

Antonio inhaled deeply. "What nags me most is that it was because of me. That really hurts. The last thing I want is to make matters worse. So I figure leaving is the only real solution."

Rubén nodded. "Where you gonna go?"

"I don't know yet. But I'll let you know as soon as we figure it out."

"That's probably a good idea—going far away, I mean."

"I think so."

"When do you wanna move in?"

"A couple of days, I guess. I haven't told John yet."

CHAPTER 18

John moved slowly, as if tired or preoccupied with his own thoughts, when Stacey pulled into his driveway and said goodnight. Without saying a word, he managed to open the passenger side door and pull himself out. When he finally turned around, he tried to project some charm.

"Are you ladies sure you don't wanna come in and relax for a bit?"

"Thank you," said Stacey, "but it's getting late. I'm sure Maria and Raul need to get up early tomorrow."

Maria smiled.

"Of course," said John. He cursed his imprudence. "I'll talk to you soon."

"Yes," said Maria. "Tomorrow."

They said goodnight once again, before John shut the passenger door. The car backed out of the driveway and disappeared into the night.

John stood there, musing over the evening highlights, before going inside.

He took off his jacket and poured himself a glass of wine, before walking over to the grand piano. Closing his eyes, he let his fingers glide over the keys in a back-and-forth motion, as if trying to tease out the melody.

He reached for a sip of wine, then played a few rusty notes. Then a few more.

Before he knew it, he was playing Beethoven's "Für Elise"—Beth's favorite!

He suddenly froze, looking up at his wineglass.

The wine lost its glamour. But not its effect, he hoped.

He considering it carefully, before gulping it down.

Then he went straight to bed.

Chapter 19

With the previous night cut short, Stacey never got the opportunity to speak with Antonio about the future. And in a case like this, specifics meant everything. She spent most of the night twisting and turning, barely catching three hours of sleep before the alarm went off.

Only the prospect of hope dragged her to a cold shower that finally woke her up. Then the racing thoughts continued. By the time she finished dressing, the anxious buildup tempted her to go out for a run, but it was too late for that.

She called Antonio, instead, hoping to catch him before he left for work.

John passed the phone to Antonio.

"You wanna go out to dinner tonight?" said Stacey. "Just you and me?"

"Where did you have in mind?"

"Don't worry. We'll find a safe place."

"Sounds great. There's some things we should talk about."

"My feelings exactly."

Stacey ate a quick breakfast and drank her coffee on the way to the office.

With no one as an outlet to share her thoughts, she struggled to maintain her sanity throughout the morning. The last thing she needed was someone picking up on her emotional struggle and spreading more rumors.

She didn't know who to trust anymore.

As soon as lunch came around, she headed straight for John's classroom, bringing the overflow of energy with her.

"So," said Stacey, "you ready to see Maria tonight?"

"Of course."

"Are you sure?"

"It's not like you and Antonio gave me much of a choice."

"No, no, no." She waved her index finger at John. "*You* got yourself into tonight's mess. And quite voluntarily, I might add."

John grinned. "I suppose I did."

"You most certainly did." She leaned over his desk. "Do you have any idea what it's like to feel the way I've been feeling all morning and not be able to share with anyone?"

"You mean about last night—you and Antonio?"

Stacey nodded.

"I can imagine."

"I've been wanting to talk to you all morning," she said. "I just don't think I can wait 'til the end of the year anymore. I need to get out of here now. Before I go mad."

John leaned back in his chair. "Sounds like you've made up your mind."

"Pretty much."

"You and Antonio gonna talk it over tonight?"

"That's what I had in mind."

"Well," He tried to console himself. "Think it over carefully."

CHAPTER 20

Slowly but surely, the afternoon became burdened with fog, making it impossible for Antonio and Jack to continue their work in the fields. They sent Rogelio home early and set to work on the foundation frame for Max's shack, hoping to have it ready for the cement pouring the following day.

Antonio brought Jack up to date concerning Stacey.

"Wait 'til I tell Anne!" said Jack.

"Just keep it to yourselves. We can't afford any more rumors."

As Antonio cut some additional two-by-fours, the sound of crackling gravel turned their attention to the driveway. When a car came into view, they recognized Stacey and went to meet her.

"And don't make any comments about her eye patch," said Antonio.

"Don't worry."

Stacey gave them both a hug.

"Whatta you doing here so early?" said Antonio.

"I came straight from school. I thought we could get an early start on dinner."

"I don't know." He turned to Jack. "We've put off that foundation long enough."

Stacey smiled. "You don't mind, do you, Jack?"

"Absolutely not! I know a priority when I see one."

"You see," said Stacey.

"Besides," said Jack. "Antonio told me you guys need ta talk. Where you goin'?"

"That's a surprise."

Stacey hooked her arm around Antonio's.

"I promise I'll come back after dinner and finish," said Antonio.

"Don't worry. We can do it tomorrow."

"That's the only way I can feel good about leaving early."

"Seriously, don't sweat it."

Stacey tugged at Antonio's arm. "We'll see you later, Jack."

"Be careful. There's a lot of fog out there."

They hopped in her car and drove off.

· · · · · · · · · · · · · · · ·

"So where we going?" said Antonio.

"I told you—it's a surprise."

"Oh, come on."

"I'll tell you," she said, taking her eyes off the fog-ridden road, "but only if you promise to run away with me."

Antonio chuckled. "Is that a bribe?"

"If that's what you wanna call it." She kept her eyes on him, intent on getting an answer.

"Okay, okay," said Antonio. "Just keep your eyes on the road. Otherwise, we won't get the opportunity."

She conceded with a smile. "I'm serious."

"I figured."

"And I was thinking *soon*."

"How soon?" said Antonio.

"As soon as we break for Christmas."

Antonio remained silent, assessing the plan in his mind.

"You're not having second thoughts, are you?" said Stacey.

"Of course not. It's just funny how things work out. I was gonna propose the same thing. I just wasn't sure about the timing."

"The sooner, the better, as far as I'm concerned."

"As a matter of fact, I just spoke to my brother about staying with him for a while. I figure that would be less suspicious than you disappearing all of a sudden."

"You're probably right. Maybe it'll cool off Don, knowing you're not around anymore."

"Hopefully. But we need to go far away."

"That's fine with me."

"You probably won't see anyone for a long time."

She reached out to Antonio. "As long as I'm with you, it doesn't matter."

He took her hand. "You still haven't told me where we're going."

"Old Sacramento."

"Really?" He sat up straight.

"You see, now you spoiled the surprise."

"Not at all," said Antonio. "It must be twenty years since I've been there."

"Really?"

"Yes. It was one of our school trips, remember?"

"Oh, *that one*." She poked fun at him. "That was *way* back—before you had the guts to open up to me."

"You gonna rub it in again?"

"Of course."

. . . .

With less fog to contend with in Old Sacramento, they strolled through the delightful array of nineteenth century architecture, which now hosted a variety of museums, shops, and restaurants. The broadboard sidewalks and overhanging balconies further transported them in time. They sauntered along, enjoying some window shopping, until one antique shop in particular caught their attention. They were admiring some Native American jewelry, when Stacey looked at her watch and beckoned Antonio along.

She scurried forth with Antonio behind her. "Whatta you up to now?"

"It's a surprise," she said.

"Another surprise?"

She asked him to close his eyes and guided him along as best she could. They crossed the street on the heels of a horse and carriage. Around the corner of Fourth Street, she found an available carriage and quietly negotiated a tour.

"Open your eyes," she said.

Antonio smiled from ear to ear.

"I thought it'd be romantic to go on a little ride before dinner," she said.

"Let's do it!"

He helped Stacey onto the carriage and joined her. She cuddled next to him.

The carriage driver cracked his whip, inspiring the horse's clanking over the cobblestone streets. As if on cue, the streetlamps lit up in response to the fading, evening sky.

"Oh, my gosh!" said Stacey. "How perfect."

Antonio took it all in. "Do you really remember that fieldtrip we took?"

"How could I forget?"

"All I remember is having lunch in front of the Railroad Depot." Then he pointing to the Delta King Hotel and Restaurant, a restored steamboat from the 1800s, still afloat on the bank of the Sacramento River. "*That* I don't remember at all."

"Well, hopefully, you'll remember much more after tonight."

. . . .

"You can open your eyes now," said Stacey.

Spanish-brick walls gracefully held up the wooden, high-beam ceiling of Los Nopales Restaurant, while arched windows added to the intimate atmosphere of low-hanging fans and functional dinner balconies—one on each side wall—overlooking the restaurant floor.

"Wow!" said Antonio, inhaling the *chile* aroma that filled the air. "Someone really knew what they were doing when they designed this place."

"I thought you'd like it."

They asked for a table on one of the balconies.

Antonio ordered *chile relleno*.

"They have good *albondigas*," said Stacey.

"Really?"

He changed his order.

Stacey ordered the *chile relleno* so he could try it anyway.

When the food arrived, they shared.

"These *are* great *albondigas*," said Antonio.

"I was gonna make some for you the other day," said Stacey, "before we went looking for Maria Lopez."

"Really?"

"Yes, really."

Antonio waved the aromas of his plate to his nose. "Good thing you didn't tell me. Otherwise, John wouldn't be visiting Maria right now."

Stacey laughed.

"You know," she said, "you still haven't given me a good explanation for taking so long to open up to me back in school. I was afraid I'd have to force your hand."

Antonio reflected as he glanced over the balcony rail. "Maybe it was for the same reason I wouldn't jump into the pool that one time during swimming lessons. I wasn't too sure of myself back then. Maybe I was afraid. I don't know."

"But we're all insecure at that age."

"True."

She put down her fork, waiting for a better explanation. "I'd almost given up on you by the ninth grade."

"Really?"

"Think about it. The only thing we had in common was playing soccer at recess. But that all changed in high school. All of a sudden, I couldn't approach you without an excuse. I even wondered if you felt anything for me at all. You never really told me."

Antonio wiped himself with his napkin. "I'm sorry. I just wasn't very good at expressing myself. You saw how difficult it was for me to finally say something."

"Yes." She gazed into his eyes. "You were so sweet; I was beside myself."

"You could've permanently scarred me if you wanted?"

He glanced away.

"What's the matter?" said Stacey.

"Don't you remember?"

"Of course, I remember."

"I felt like such a coward."

"Nooo!" She reached for his hand. "On the contrary, I thought you were quite brave?"

"Brave? For what? Beating myself up emotionally?"

"No!" She gripped his hand more firmly. "For forcing yourself to break out of your emotional box."

"You were real patient with me. I remember that."

"I understood more than you gave me credit for. I was pretty boxed in myself."

"Anyone else might've ridiculed me."

"Well, *I* knew better," she said with a smile.

"I still can't believe I waited 'til the last day of school to say something."

"No kidding!" said Stacey. "Then I didn't see you for the entire summer."

"That's right." Antonio chuckled. "I didn't have a car."

"That part's not so funny."

"I'm sorry." He tried to control himself.

"You *were* nervous, though?"

"Of course, I was nervous. What'd you expect? I don't even remember how I managed to pull you away from your friends. All I knew is that I couldn't keep putting it off. Then it seemed that, no matter how hard I tried, I couldn't get the words out of my mouth."

He pursed his lips. "I was getting on my own nerves for being so pitiful."

"Don't say that."

"I forced it out. It just didn't come across as romantically as I hoped."

"You were precious," said Stacey.

"If you say so."

"At least you were yourself. I was so consumed with being a people pleaser that I hardly knew how to be me. Why do you think I got so good at soccer?"

Antonio gave her a blank look. "You never told me that."

"You must've had some idea."

Antonio remained silent.

"Anyway, you're the one who helped me break out of my own shell—once you finally opened up to me. My parents certainly noticed. And I have to tell you, they didn't appreciate my newly-found assertiveness one bit. I'm pretty sure they blamed you for it."

Antonio snickered. "That explains a few things."

"At least, with no more soccer, you couldn't boss us around the field anymore."

"Boss you around?"

"Good thing I knew there was more to you than that. I just had to tease it out of you."

"Well, that you did," said Antonio.

. . . .

The fog had thickened by the time Antonio and Stacey strolled out of Los Nopales Restaurant. Streetlamps probed through the evening mist, guiding the two once again along the canopied, broad-board sidewalks. They walked side by side, taking in the remaining sights, without a care in the world.

"Guess where I'm taking you next," said Stacey.

"Next? You had quite an evening planned, didn't you?"

"You'll like this place. It's quite peculiar." She pointed as they came around the corner. "That's it over there—Fanny Ann's Saloon."

Once inside, Antonio understood what she meant by "peculiar." Someone had papered the ceiling and some of the walls with colorful, old magazine pages. The real charm, however, consisted of industrial revolution paraphernalia that hung from the ceiling, including an early model motorcycle, an old horse-drawn buggy, and a crowded assortment of outdated farming tools and machinery.

"This place reminds me of Foster's Bighorn," said Antonio. "Just different stuff."

"Yes," said Stacey, "it kind of does."

"What can I get for you?" said the bartender.

Antonio suggested an Irish coffee so Stacey could keep warm. She seemed to like the idea, so he ordered one for himself.

"You're sweet as ever," said Stacey. "Always trying to please me."

"Oh, I've changed," Antonio bantered.

"*You* know what I mean." She bumped his side. "I, on the other hand, I'm afraid I've hardened over the years."

"You've been through a lot."

"I suppose. It's part of our human nature, right? The struggle to reconcile the past through the present." She paused. "But does it ever end?"

"Not as long as there's a past that needs reconciling." The bartender delivered their coffees. "Korea, for example. That's why I have a hard time dealing with injustice—always feeling that I need to do something about it."

"Do we need to go there again?" said Stacey.

"No. It's just that I hate when I create more problems than I solve. That's all."

He took a sip of his coffee.

"Hold it right there!" said Stacey. "Didn't you just tell me not to be so hard on myself?"

The empathy drew him to Stacey like a magnet. He reached out and took hold of her hand, before drawing it slowly to his lips.

"Wow," said Stacey. "I should complain more often."

"Don't push your luck," said Antonio.

"With unrestrained affection like that, how can you blame me for loving you?"

"Well," said Antonio, "having lived with myself my whole life, I'd have to say that I don't know. But that's the beauty of it, I guess—recognizing how much God loves us and allowing His love to flow through us—even as He helps us deal with our own shortcomings."

Stacey beamed at him with a smile.

"What?" said Antonio.

"Nothing," she said. "Only that you would've made a good priest."

CHAPTER 21

Don drove his gray BMW with indignation, as far back as possible, without losing sight of Stacey's car through the thick of the fog. He wished he could run them off the road. That would make an end of it. It enraged him—that they could expect to get away with going behind his back, just because they went out of town. What an insult to his intelligence.

He reckoned Stacey must not have learned her lesson, after all.

Damn-it! It was just like her.

He did his best to remain calm and focused. He couldn't afford any more screw-ups. Things had to be done right, once and for all.

Stacey slowed to a stop at the gravel road entrance to Jack's farm.

Don pulled off to the side and waited.

After a moment, Antonio stepped out and waved good-bye.

Stacey gave a slight honk good-bye and resumed her drive into the blinding fog.

Don immediately put his car in gear and followed her into town.

. . . .

Standing on the front porch of his parents' house, Don puffed on a cigarette, waiting for someone to open the door. His mind raced. When Sharon came, he dropped the cigarette, putting it out with his boot.

Sharon looked at him with concern. "I thought you gave up smoking, son."

"I did," he said. "Is Mike here?"

"He's in the kitchen." She motioned for him to come in.

"Mike!" he yelled.

"What's wrong?" she asked.

"Nothing," said Don. "I just came by to help him with something."

"What?" Mike answered from inside the kitchen.

"I came by to help you with that stuff you asked me about," said Don, trying to sound convincing. "Let's go. I don't have much time."

"What stuff?"

"That thing at Foster's," said Don, impatiently. "We have to leave now."

"I'm busy right now."

Don scurried through the living room and into the kitchen.

He found Mike sitting at the table, eating pie. He had removed his nose patch, giving his bruised face some air.

Don grabbed him by the arm. "Damn-it, Mike," he said in a low voice. "Stop screwin' around. I've wasted enough time looking for you already."

"So. Why right now?"

"Because it might be the only chance we get. That's why."

Mike hesitated.

"You wanna get rid of Qüintero, or not?"

Mike yanked his arm loose. "Oh, shit. That's right." He said it in a tone loud enough for Sharon to hear. "I forgot it was tonight."

CHAPTER 22

Inside the tractor shop, Antonio measured the remaining two-by-fours needed to finish the foundation frame for Max's new shed. He and Jack had already excavated and leveled off the area. The rain itself had taken care of the tamping. He just needed to pour the gravel base inside the form boards to help with the drainage, and possible freezing, during times of extreme weather. The reinforcing mesh lay by the work bench, ready for the cement pour.

Jack considered the preparation a bit excessive, but Antonio had insisted on the details. He believed in doing things right the first time. No sense in regrets. Besides, more work now meant less work later.

At least Gavin would appreciate it.

And with Max all grown up, Antonio had a feeling Jack might consider getting his son a new calf—if anything, just to fill the void Max had left with his rapid growth. With any luck, Antonio figured Max might get a female companion. So the only way to provide for an uncertain future was to build a shed that could easily accommodate an extra occupant.

A sudden rush of fatigue came over Antonio.

Perhaps he had eaten too much. Or maybe it was just getting too cold? He considered calling it a night. He had done enough work for one evening, anyway.

Max shook his head and snorted from the opposite side of the workbench.

"I'm glad I'm not the only one complaining," said Antonio. "Maybe I should let you get some sleep now. Whatta you think?"

He went over and stroked Max's neck.

"Your new home should be done in a few days. You getting excited?"

The bull shook itself loose.

"Am I the only one who cares, or what?"

Max ignored him, tromping his way out of the shop.

"Where you going, Max? Am I boring you, or something?"

The bull continued in disregard.

"That's gratitude for you. Just for that I'm not leaving 'till I finish."

Antonio smiled and set himself back to work.

CHAPTER 23

Don turned off his headlights and drove up quietly under a series of tall, semi-bare cottonwood trees, where both he and Mike could see the radiating yellow light over the tractor shop entrance. It pierced the thick fog for a good forty-yard radius, while a florescent light emanated from within the shop itself.

"Qüintero must be inside," said Don.

"So whatta we do?"

Don glared at Mike. "We wait and make sure. We can't afford any more screw-ups. What the hell do they teach you in the Army, anyway? This isn't much different from a building search?"

Mike bit his jaw, clearly miffed.

. . . .

Eternity seems like never enough time when in good company, and by the same token, even a few seconds could feel like forever with someone you don't particularly like. Every passing minute feels like an untreated wound, slowly rotting away with infection. Eventually, gangrene sets in and amputation becomes a necessary evil.

Mike had become a master of self-distraction. When he remembered, he could do the smallest thing and forget whatever troubled him. He took his index finger and explored his bruised face. He felt around, trying to figure out if there was any change in the pain perimeter since he last checked.

Nothing. No change.

At least the cold weather continued its numbing effect.

"There he is!" Don pointed. "Inside. You see him?"

Mike looked up and about, trying to orient himself.

"Yeah, I see him."

"Well, now we know where he is. Go do it."

Mike felt a sudden cramp down his spinal column and all the way to his ankle, flashing back to the force that toppled him at Foster's.

"What the hell you waitin' for?" said Don.

Mike shook off the image and reached for the door handle. His heart raced. He closed his eyes, imagining what it would be like to inflict damage on Qüintero for a change.

Once satisfied, he reached for a steel rod, squeezing it hard for reassurance.

He slipped out of the car, without paying attention to the last-minute instructions Don gave him. And when he finally noticed Don's lips moving, it never occurred to him to stop and listen. He closed the door behind him, without clicking it shut. It would make it easier, in case he needed to make a quick get-away.

With the chill of the night, he wondered if he should've worn an extra layer. A bit too late for that. He felt the air begin to burn his sinus with every breath.

He focused on slower, deeper breathing.

Walking on haunches, he kept his eyes on the entrance to the shop, occasionally looking down to maintain his footing.

He rolled the steel rod in his hand to pacify himself.

At one point he looked back at the car, only to see Don pointing, in frustration, at the shop—in an effort to keep him moving.

He rolled the rod in his hand more quickly, wondering for the first time why they hadn't strategized a two-pronged maneuver. If the fog light above the shop exposed him more than expected, he might not be able to stalk Qüintero by himself.

Why didn't they make contingency plans?

The sound of sawing from inside the shop brought him back to attention.

He took a deep breath, with his heart still pounding, as he scurried for the cover of a nearby tree. Considering his next move, he spotted a peculiar structure on the ground. A curious, cautionary confusion took over. He squatted down to examine the contraption, only to realize it had to be some kind of foundation frame.

Relieved that it was nothing, he rose to his feet and gave it a kick, popping out one of the corner joints that remained loose.

The two-by-fours protested with a noticeable thunk.

Mike cursed himself.

He dropped to his stomach for cover, clinging to the ground with his fingertips.

The sudden dive jolted his body, making his bruised face thunder with pain. He curled up like a worm—hands to his face—trying to focus on his breathing.

The throbbing kept him glued to the ground and out of sight.

He alternated between anger and frustration, aching to lash out at something, until the pain slowly subsided and the sawing from inside the shop began to filter through again. At least he hadn't blown his cover.

He picked himself up, once again setting his sights on the tractor shop entrance.

When he glanced back at the car, Don had his arms spread out in horror. Then he mouthed something off with passion, as he continued to point in the direction of the shop.

Mike ignored him, twirling the rod in his hand.

The motion renewed some anticipation.

As he continued his left flank a rusty cultivator lay strewn to the side, with a ribbing plow half-buried next to it, alerting him to proceed with caution.

When he reached the corner of the shop, the sawing inside suddenly stopped.

He feared that Qüintero might exit the shop before he could move into position. That would render their plan worthless.

And what if he had to make a quick getaway? How was he supposed to manage? That's another detail they hadn't anticipated.

Mike made a fist with his free hand. Don better not leave without him.

Something rattled from behind.

Mike froze. It couldn't be Qüintero. He hadn't come out of the shop.

A chill raised the hairs on his neck.

Expecting the worst, he tightened his grip on the steel rod.

As he swung around, there before him—no more than twenty yards away—stood an enormous, black bull.

Mike's heart sank.

He almost dropped the rod.

His instinct told him to run, but his military training kept him in place.

He held his breath, tilting his gaze to the left and to the right.

The bull's eyes blazed from the yellow light above the shop, questioning Mike's trespass with a snorting swing of the head.

When Mike made a leaning motion to the right, the bull gestured in kind.

Mike froze, fretting over his next move.

He wanted to look over at Don, as a petition for help, but he couldn't risk even that.

He had to run for it. There seemed no other way.

He swung the rod over his head, hurling it at the bull's face with all his strength. The clash made the bull roll its neck with a horrendous sounding bellow.

Mike turned and jetted toward the back of the shop.

As soon as the bull shook off the blow, it thundered after him.

Mike ran—as if airborne.

As he came around the corner, a rotary hoe materialized through the darkness. He jerked his weight to the side as one of the blades scraped his right thigh, almost knocking him to the ground. He cursed life itself as the bull shook the ground behind him.

Regaining his footing, he took note of a heap of alfalfa bales ahead.

He dashed toward the promising haven.

With two large strides, he jumped over two bales, then a third.

Right behind him, the bull slammed the alfalfa heap with full force.

Mike wobbled, almost losing his grip on the thick plastic that covered the heap, yet somehow, he managed to reassert himself and crawl to the top.

The bull pulled back, ramming a second time—not quite as strongly—but Mike could feel the alfalfa packs coming apart.

He heard Qüintero coming around the side of the shop.

"What the heck are you doing, Max?"

Mike looked ahead, wondering where to jump. If he ran around the other side of the shop, he might make it to the car. Except for a walnut tree, he had a clean jump.

As he squatted, the bull's rumbling force shook him again.

With a frustrated tilt of the head, Mike steadied himself and took the leap.

He hit the ground running.

It didn't take the bull long to figure things out.

Mike made it around the corner. He could see the shop light behind the corn harvester. In a surge of hope, he flew around at breakneck speed.

Then he heard the bull come around the corner.

What the hell! If only he had a gun. He could turn around and take it down right there. There was no way he'd make it to the car in time.

And where the hell was Don? He must've seen he was in trouble.

Mike suddenly regretted everything.

The bull pounded the ground behind him as tears forced their way through his lacrimal ducts.

He noticed a mound up ahead. It was well lit from the light above the shop.

It might give him the time he needed, while the bull scrambled around.

He went straight for it, gaging every stride, before jumping with all his might.

He landed solidly, without losing speed.

In just a few more seconds he'd be on his way, so he expected Don to be ready.

Mike heard the bull taking the right side of the mound.

He compensated to the left.

"Maaax!" yelled Qüintero.

Mike kept running for his life.

Detecting a good jumping-off point, he measured his paces, planting his right foot and throwing himself forward.

When he saw the thin-spiked harrow within the shadow of the mound, it was too late.

All of a sudden, it seemed that time slowed down, and something like a magnetic field buzzed all around him, making him self-conscious of every microsecond as he flew across the air. He almost convinced himself that he could glide, looking up at the cottonwood trees, where Don lay waiting.

Mike's face cringed as his left foot landed on the first spike. It punctured his shoe like jelly, stabbing the sole of his foot, right through the bones. With his right leg still flying high from the momentum, his impaled foot yanked and crunched apart the cuneiform bones.

He swung his hands forward in desperation, turning his head to the side, as his mouth gaped open with a shrieking cry. He tried to break the fall, but his left hand slipped between the spikes as the rest of his body landed on them with full-force.

He lay there, wide-eyed and motionless.

The spikes through his abdomen didn't seem to bother him. It was the one making his heart cramp that didn't feel so good.

He tried to lift his head, but a spike through his left eye socket held it in place.

The bull stopped its chase.

Approaching footsteps suddenly replaced it.

"'elp," said Mike.

Qüintero reached out to caress Mike's head.

Mike sensed the significance, and a remorseful terror jolted his body. He wanted to apologize, but his remaining eye weighed him down with fatigue. He considered fighting it, but death was the path of least resistance, and with that he found rest.

· · · · · · · · · · · · · · · · · · · ·

Antonio clenched his eyes in disbelief.

Just then, a car engine started up from under the cottonwood trees.

Antonio spun around. A car sped off into the fog. He considered chasing after it, but he knew he'd never catch it.

Instead, he sat over Mike and prayed.

When he finally got up, he went straight to the phone inside the tractor shop. He dialed 9-1-1 and asked for an ambulance. They asked him what happened. He explained it was an accident. They asked for details. They wanted to make sure Mike was dead. Of course, he was dead. He fell on some farm equipment. What kind of farm equipment? What the heck did that matter? Were they gonna send an ambulance, or not? They told him it was on its way.

He hung up and called Jack. Jack told him he'd be right over.

He considered calling John, but there was no point in ruining his evening. There was nothing he could do anyway.

He went outside and waited.

Max saw him and approached with caution.

Antonio noticed the blood on Max's face. One of his eyes was cut and swollen. It must've been a heck of a blow. No wonder he was after Mike. But who could imagine something like that could happen at this time of night?

He took Max inside the shop, then searched outside, looking for anything that could help him sort things out.

CHAPTER 24

As soon as Don heard the 9-1-1 dispatch, he picked up the police radio and called for Officer Albert McCabe, who was currently on watch.

"This is Al, chief," he answered informally. "What's got you up so late?"

"Where you at, Al?"

"By the baseball park. I was just on my way to the Smith farm."

"Pick me up at the station."

"Did you hear the call?"

"Yeah. Pick me up at the station. I have a bad feeling about this."

. . . .

The police station occupied the same building as the courtroom and City Hall, right at the end of Main Street and close to the riverbank. Don was already waiting by the time McCabe swung by. He motioned for McCabe to hurry up and jumped into the patrol vehicle.

"What's up, chief?"

Don stared through the windshield, as if unable to turn.

"Mike told me he was gonna go see Qüintero tonight. He wanted to talk and get over the bad blood he'd been feelin'."

"At this time a night?"

"No. Earlier. That's what worries me about the call."

"Whatta you mean?"

He turned to Albert. "I haven't heard from Mike."

CHAPTER 25

Jack's pickup flew into the gravel driveway, before coming to a scratching halt. His face remained expressionless as he grabbed his rifle and stormed toward Antonio.

"Where the hell's Max?"

"In the shop," said Antonio

Jack threw open the sliding door with Antonio behind him.

As Max looked up from a lying position, Jack raised his rifle.

He pointed it between Max's eyes—about to fire—when Antonio reached from behind and pulled the barrel to the side.

"Whatta you doing?" said Antonio.

"What's it look like?"

"You can't shoot him. It wasn't Max's fault."

"I'm not about ta wait for another accident."

"Everything'll be fine as soon as we finish that shed."

"Screw the shed. It's too late for that."

"Look," said Antonio, "tomorrow you can do whatever you want. I won't stop you. Just think it over first, will you? Besides, that's evidence on Max's face."

CHAPTER 26

Despite the fog, the ambulance lights almost blinded Don and McCabe as they pulled onto the gravel road entrance to Jack Smith's farm. They coasted by the other night watch officer, Barry Miller, and the paramedics, who examined Mike's body and shuffled methodically about, making sure they exhausted all possible life-saving measures.

Antonio and Jack remained at a distance by the tractor shop entrance.

The patrol vehicle pulled up next to the ambulance, where Don and McCabe could better assess the situation. As they emerged from the vehicle and approached the scene, the paramedics suddenly stopped looking busy—hovering in silence over Mike's body.

After a prolonged pause, Officer Miller looked up at Don.

Don remained silent.

"I'm sorry," said Miller.

Don gave no sign of emotion.

With mounting unease one of the paramedics picked himself up and approached Don, putting one hand on his shoulder and giving him a consoling pat with the other. It was all he could do. Mike was dead, and nothing more could be done about it.

He turned and grabbed his trauma bag, before heading back to the ambulance.

The other paramedic took his airway bag and consoled McCabe. It was obviously an awkward moment for the young medic—acknowledging Mike's death—especially since Mike had gone to school with McCabe's younger brother.

The medic pulled himself away and went to join his partner. They chatted inside the ambulance, watching the officers take some forensic pictures, before driving back to town.

When the coroner arrived, he and his assistant got briefed by the officers, then proceeded with the mechanical task of removing Mike's body.

Antonio and Jack observed at a distance.

After loading the body, the coroner waved good-bye and disappeared into the fog.

. . . .

The shop's yellow fog light fell on everyone like an electric hailstorm.

Don didn't move for a while.

McCabe and Miller waited for instructions, while Antonio and Jack looked at one another with mounting displeasure.

Don turned in the direction of the bloody harrow. He had to remind himself that Mike was only a body now. He needed to keep that straight in his head and not let it affect his judgment. He needed to follow through. Otherwise, Mike's death would be for nothing, and he sure as hell couldn't let that happen.

"You have anything to say about this, Qüintero?" said Don, finally.

Antonio jumbled back to reality.

He looked up with a scowl. "No, I don't. Why? You wanna tell me something?"

"I wanna know what happened here." Don looked over at Officer Miller. "Why don't you take a few more pictures, Barry."

"Sure," said Miller. But he hesitated. "Why don't you go home, chief. Albert and I can take care of things here."

"I ain't goin' anywhere. Not 'til this is resolved." He looked over at Antonio. "What happened, Qüintero?"

"I was inside the shop. I missed most of it myself."

"What the hell do you mean you missed most of it?"

"Exactly what I said. I was inside the shop. I heard Max— that's the bull. He was making a racket outside. When I came out, I heard him running around the back. I chased after him, but I didn't realize what was happening until right before Mike fell on the harrow." He paused. "There was nothing I could do. That's when I called 9-1-1."

"So you had nothing to do with this," said Don.

"That's right."

"Then what happened to the few hours Mike was here for?"

Antonio scowled anew. "What few hours?"

"He told me he was comin' to talk things over with you. He didn't like the way he'd been feelin' about things."

"I don't know anything about that. The first I saw of him was right before he fell."

Don looked him over. "That's a pretty convenient story when there's no one to corroborate it." He squinched at the implication of his words. Then he looked over at Jack. "Were *you* here when it happened?"

"No. He called me right after. But I didn't need ta be here ta know that nephew of yours wouldn't apologize if his life depended on it."

Don stared at him fiercely. "Nobody's asking your opinion, Jack."

"I really don't give a damn. I'm givin' it to ya anyway."

Don ignored him by turning to Antonio. "What was it you said about that bull?"

"What the hell does the bull have ta do with anything?" said Jack. "It doesn't know why Mike came over."

Don turned around, waving a threatening finger. "If you don't shut up and let me conduct my business, I'll have you escorted to the back of that patrol vehicle, you hear?"

"Yeah, yeah," said Jack in a more subdued tone.

Don prompted Antonio. "You were saying."

"The bull was chasing after Mike," Antonio repeated.

"When he fell on the harrow?"

"Yes."

Don gave him a suspicious glare. "So the bull killed him. It's the bull's fault, right?"

"No," said Antonio firmly. "Mike provoked it."

"Provoked it? How?"

"I found a steel rod that he bashed its face with."

"You saw this?"

"No! I told you I was inside the shop."

"Then how do you know?"

"Look at the bull's face. He's inside the shop."

McCabe peered through the sliding door. "I see a rod on the workbench."

When he slid open the door, the bull came into full view. It stared right at him.

"Holy shit." said McCabe. "That's a big bull."

Don walked up to the sliding door and sneered. "That doesn't look like a rod wound to me."

He drew out his pistol, aiming right at Max's face, and fired before anyone could say a word. Max bellowed a heinous roar as he collapsed to the ground, with his eyes grotesquely rolled back, followed by violent kicking and convulsions.

"What the hell ya think ya're doin'?" said Jack.

"I figure he's caused enough problems for one day," said Don.

Antonio rushed into the shop. "What was that for?"

"It's better this way."

"Says who?"

"Says me." He gave Antonio a dirty look. "Maybe now you can focus on giving me some straight answers."

"That *was* a rod wound before you shot him," said Antonio.

"Let me get this straight. You still expect this bull to be your alibi? A dead bull, for that matter. Is that correct?"

"Mike provoked it!"

"Why don't you put up some tape, Al. Section off the area."

It took McCabe a couple seconds to refocus.

"Sure, chief." He walked over to the patrol vehicle, grabbed some crime tape from the trunk, and went to work.

"Tell me," said Don. "Why would Mike wanna attack this bull? That's what I wanna know."

"How would I know? I just heard the ruckus. I'm sure Max wasn't bellowing out of pleasure."

"Look, why don't you cut the crap? I don't think the bull's gonna give us any answers."

"Well, I'd have to agree with you on that."

"Your statement isn't helping much either."

"Maybe you're not asking the right questions."

Don's face stiffened. "What the hell's that supposed to mean?" He scrutinized Antonio. "You tryin' to tell me how to do my job?"

"No," said Antonio, "only that Mike wasn't the only one here."

Don's brows went up. "Huh?"

"When I came up to Mike—after he fell on the harrow—a car took off from under those trees over there." Antonio pointed. "I'm sure they came together."

"Why do you say that?"

"It seems pretty obvious. I don't think he walked here."

Don's face lit up, and the blood rushed to his face. "Don't start getting smart with me, Qüintero."

"Then why don't you find out who brought him here? That'll provide all your answers."

Don examined him closely, unsure of whether to ask the question. "What . . . type vehicle dju see?" he mouthed weakly.

"I'm not sure. I wasn't particularly interested at the time."

"Well, that's convenient!" declared Don, with renewed confidence.

Antonio's brows narrowed. "Look, I'm not answering any more questions 'til you find out who drove off in that car."

Jack smiled profoundly at his response.

Don fidgeted at the prospect of jabbing Antonio across the stomach with his baton.

"Why the hell don't you tell me again where that vehicle was parked," he said.

Antonio pointed.

"Al." Don motioned him over. "Why don't you keep an eye on these two, while I check this out."

. . . .

McCabe put the crime tape on hold. He tried to start some casual conversation to ease the tension, but only Antonio seemed receptive. Jack elbowed him to keep an eye on Don as he walked in the direction of the cottonwood trees. They all watched as his forwardly bent outline maneuvered under the fog-filled tree limbs. For a moment, he turned off his flashlight, twisting about, before turning it back on.

He squatted, as if to pick something up.

Jack poked Antonio's side again, making sure he remained attentive.

All the while, Don twisted about some more. He switched his flashlight off and on again, stepping into a grassy area that covered him to his knees. Then he stomped around, examining the area, before heading back.

McCabe, having worked with Don for over six years, had complete confidence in his superior officer. Of course, he had his own way of doing things at times, but that was occasionally necessary. In fact, there was hardly a time when he felt he could've questioned Don's actions.

. . . .

"Are you sure that was the spot?" said Don.

"Yes, I'm sure," said Antonio.

"Well, there's nothing of interest there."

Antonio frowned. "Whatta you mean, 'nothing of interest'? Didn't you see tire tracks?"

"I mean nothing. There's nothing there that can help us with our investigation."

Antonio expelled a breath of defeat.

"If there's nothin' of interest," said Jack, "then what the hell were ya pickin' up over there?"

Don ignored the question.

"Maybe someone can check again tomorrow," said Antonio. "See if you missed anything."

"Sure," said Don, reveling in triumph, "we can do that. For whatever it's worth."

"You dirty bastard!" said Jack.

Don swung around, shoving his baton into Jack's sternum.

Jack's thin body cringed, nearly bringing him to his knees. But he seemed to tighten every muscle in his body, before pulling himself up and glaring into Don's piercing eyes.

"Albert," said Don, with a glare of his own, "shove this piece o' shit in the back seat before we have to take him in. It's for his own good."

McCabe took Jack by the arm and guided him to the patrol vehicle.

"What I wanna know," said Don, gloating over Jack, "is who's responsible for that harrow being exposed the way it is."

"I am," said Antonio, without hesitation.

Jack glared at him. "Shut the hell up, Antonio. Whatta you sayin'?"

Don laughed out loud. "What's the matter, boys? You both wanna take credit for this? That's perfectly okay with me."

Jack and Antonio probed each other's eyes.

"Barry!" Don called out.

"Yeah." The voice came from behind the tractor shop.

"Did you find any evidence of contusions with a steel rod on Mike's body?"

Officer Miller came around the side of the shop. "Nothing obvious, but it's hard to say without a thorough examination."

"Give me a break," said Antonio. "Why don't you cut the crap and get this over with."

"Anything else, Barry?" said Don.

"There *are* some foot and hoof prints around the back of the shop."

"Any post-mortem injuries that you noticed on Mike?"

"None that I could ascertain."

Don frowned. "Well, we still need to read you your rights, Qüintero."

"What the hell's the charge?" said Jack, suddenly resisting Officer McCabe from putting him in the car.

Don looked directly at Jack. "Murder," he said calmly.

"It was a damn accident, and you know it!"

"All I know," said Don, "is that we have a possible murder and a suspect with both motive and opportunity."

"What's the motive?" said Antonio.

Don counted with his fingers in annoyance. "You have a previous history with Mike, a restraining order that's been violated, reason to avenge John's injury." He threw out his arms. "You want more motives?"

Antonio shook his head in disgust.

"I didn't think so," Don smirked. "Why don't you put your hands behind your head for me."

"Don't let 'im do this ta you!" said Jack.

Antonio hesitated.

"Come on!" Don motioned with his baton. "Get 'em up. You wanna add resisting arrest?"

Antonio hesitated.

He turned to look at Jack, who was howling incomprehensibly from the back seat of the patrol vehicle at this point.

"Let me just get something from the shop," said Antonio.

"You don't need anything where you're going."

The words seemed to pierce Antonio.

"Move it!" said Don.

Without warning, Antonio dropped to the ground, swinging his left leg in a sweeping motion that fell Don to the gravel.

Don clutched his ankle as Antonio thrust himself to his feet and dashed to the cover of the fog-filled darkness in the fields.

"Al! Barry! Get that son-of-a-bitch! He's getting away!"

Both officers dropped what they were doing and bolted after Antonio.

Don limped to his feet to join the chase.

Meanwhile, Jack howled victoriously from the patrol vehicle.

CHAPTER 27

Antonio ran like a feral cat, familiar with his terrain, giving no attention to the subsiding yells behind him. He ducked when the first gunshot echoed over his head. The second ruptured the earth beside him. As his eyes adjusted, he focused on the uneven ground before him, crumbling large dirt clods under his boots and shifting his weight to keep balance.

Luckily, it hadn't rained. Otherwise, his tracks would be unmistakable—even through the thickness of the fog.

He noticed the first ditch just in time.

He jumped, crossing the next field at a slightly different angle.

When he finally looked back, the shop lights were no longer visible, although he thought he caught a glimpse of flashlights, zigzagging across the fog.

He swallowed, then exhaled quick, steamy clouds of breath.

He looked ahead, then back again.

The next field was inundated with wheat growth and showered in dew. If he crossed, he would leave an unmistakable trail. Instead, he ran along one of the ditches that led to the nearest levee road. Once on the riverbank, he knew he'd find plenty of trees and brush. From there, he could find his way to safety.

. . . .

Already out of breath, the piercing chill began to burn Don's lungs. It forced him to slow down his pace. Officers McCabe and Miller led the charge with flashlights in hand. Don kept his pistol lightly poised. His fingers and ears tingled from the cold.

McCabe turned a quick glance at Don. "You really think we need that gun?" he panted. "The guy's unarmed."

Don responded with a glare and panting of his own. "Don't you question me, Al. We've both seen what this guy can do."

Miller gave McCabe a sympathetic look before turning to Don. "You really think he did it, though?"

Don wished he could ignore the question. "I can't imagine what else could've happened. Can you?"

"I wouldn't know."

"We'll worry about that later," said Don. He took a deep breath. "Right now we need to catch our suspect. You see any more tracks?"

"Not yet."

They split up and continued their search.

At a certain point Barry bent over to get a closer look at something. Don assisted him with his own flashlight.

"I think I found some footprints!" said Barry.

McCabe circled back in their direction.

Officer Miller pointed toward the river. "Looks like he's headed that way."

They picked up their pace.

· ·

Antonio made it to the levee road, just outside the town of Isleton. When he glimpsed back, the pursuing lights had disappeared. Dead silence extended in all directions. No breeze. No nothing. Only his panting and the numbing coldness reminded him that he was still awake and threat could come at any moment.

Drawn by the profile of an imposing ash tree, he made his way down to the riverbank, where the winter smell of rotten mud accumulation permeated the flowing waters, and the fog-covered river gripped him with nostalgia.

As he neared the river's edge, something snagged his boot.

Stooping over, he discovered an abandoned fishing line with the end securely tied around an empty tin can—just like the ones he used as a kid.

He picked it up out of instinct, feeling an immediate pulse on the line.

It couldn't be the current.

He balanced the line on his index finger and felt two more consecutive pulls. That had to be a fish. No doubt about it.

He reeled the line around the tin can, and there at the end, a six-inch striped bass flopped back and forth, struggling to unleash itself. Antonio took it by the gills and pulled out the hook. For a moment, he struggled with his childhood dilemma of wanting to keep it, despite the fact that it didn't meet the legal requirements.

After some reflection, he took it with both hands and reached out into the water. It struggled for a few seconds, until its slippery scales helped it slither away.

If only fish had memories to learn from their gaffs.

Antonio sat down and observed the ruffling waters—small crescents rising, then slowly rolling over and splashing against the bank. They soothed him, reminding him of his parents and his childhood. The farm. The fishing.

It all seemed so distant now. Distant and gone.

Although not everything.

Through the hypnotizing rhythm of the waves, he remembered his brother. Yes, when they were young. The way he taught Rubén to create levee roadways outside their house on the farm—next to the wooden steps leading up to the front door. If there was plenty of anything, it was dirt to build a nice levee road system for their toy cars.

What a heck of a thing to remember.

Of course, Rubén's engineering mind soon outgrew Antonio's building techniques. One day in particular, Rubén jumped into a dry ditch and carved mazes of tunnel roads into its sides, leaving Antonio utterly amazed. He even helped Rubén measure some thin pieces of wood to use as bridges from one side of the ditch to the other; and together, they built an operational network out of a dry, worthless ditch.

The sudden rustling and hushed voices coming from the other side of the levee road snapped Antonio back to attention.

Upset at letting himself get distracted, he scanned about, gauging his surroundings.

Feeling all out of options, he slipped into the bone-chilling river, where the heavy current almost dragged him off. He clutched his way through tule reeds as a shudder pulsated through his body, and he finally settled under some partially immersed, copious shrubs.

The waves sloshed at his face—like an ice pick, tearing away at his skin.

He spread his legs wide and held onto the shrubbery for stability.

A deep languor began to set in, and with it, his will to escape.

There seemed nowhere else to go—not even his brother in Sacramento. They would surely look for him there. Besides, he couldn't compromise the family.

There had to be another way.

And what was he supposed to tell Stacey? He had to leave. There was no way around it. Just not before getting word to her.

Hopefully, John would understand this time.

But what about Jack? He couldn't let him take the fall.

He just laid there—despondent—trapped like a miserable rat.

. . . .

Don remained steady with his gun, eager for the opportunity to use it, as Officers McCabe and Miller carefully swept their flashlights along the riverbank.

They occasionally stopped and listened, hoping to hear some rustling.

Barry picked up a rock and threw it into the brush.

"I don't know what to tell you, chief," said Miller.

Don sneered painfully and motioned him to keep his voice down.

Miller whispered, "This is close to where he must've come. But he could be anywhere by now. Up river, down river, even across the river."

"Shit!" That was not what Don wanted to hear. And with Barry having given away their position, he might as well put his gun away. Whatever chances they had of finding Antonio were now gone.

He looked out at the river in defeat.

"We came close," said Miller.

Don wanted to scream into his face for having exposed their position. Instead, he told them to keep looking for another hour—just out of spite. "I'm going back to take Jack in."

"Don't worry, chief," said McCabe. "We've got everything under control here. You gonna be okay?"

"I'll be fine."

. . . .

Officer Miller kicked the ground in front of him. "I don't know about you, Al, but I'm gettin' back as soon as he's far enough ahead of us. This is bullcrap. The way that guy was running, he's long gone by now. No point in freezing our butts out here."

McCabe nodded in agreement.

They threw a few more rocks into the shrub—to stay warm more than anything—keeping an eye on the retreating flashlight and cursing the fact that it wasn't moving fast enough.

As soon as the light disappeared, they headed back to the farm.

CHAPTER 28

Don knocked on John's front door as he puffed long and hard on his cigarette, watching the ashes burn extra bright in the protracted darkness. His boots and slacks still dribbled with filth from the long search out in the fields and ditches. He shook one boot with indignation, trying to break off the dried mud.

With no answer after the second knock, he pounded on the door, until John answered from inside.

"I said I'm coming! Who is it?"

"The police."

John opened the door, still trying to tie his robe.

"Whatta *you* want so early?"

"I wanna know where Qüintero is." He blew out a puff of smoke.

"What the hell for?"

"He killed Mike last night."

The cold draft seemed to freeze John in place. And despite the movement of his lips, the words refused to formulate. He just stared at Don.

"What are you talking about?" he said, finally. "He was working at the farm."

"That's where it happened."

John shook his head. "What happened?"

"Mike got thrown on some farm equipment that stabbed and killed him."

John turned silent.

"He's on the run," said Don. "Why the hell do you think I'm looking like this? We've been on his trail all night."

John looked over Don's dirty clothes.

"Looks like your boy really did it this time." Don felt satisfied that he'd gotten John's attention.

"You'll never catch him."

Don snarled. "What was that?"

"I said I didn't hear him come in."

Don let out another whisp of smoke.

"I didn't think you had." He scrutinized John. "I just wanted to give you fair warning, since I know he *will* contact you sooner or later. Remember, aiding and abetting is a serious offence. Jack found out today. He's in jail as we speak. I'm hoping we don't have to do the same with you."

John glowered.

"Do we have an understanding?"

John did not answer.

"Good," said Don. He puffed on his cigarette. "We'll be seeing you around. And make sure Stacey understands the severity of the situation. I don't think you'd like to see her get in trouble over this either."

He gave a smirk and left.

. . . .

As soon as Don drove off, John picked up the phone and called Anne to find out what she knew. He woke her, but she quickly came to her senses.

"Oh, my God," said Anne. There was a moment of silence. "He told me there was a problem at the farm, but I had no idea. Is he okay?"

"Yes, he's fine."

"What about Antonio?"

John regretted calling.

"I don't know," he said. "There must've been an accident. I was hoping *you* would know."

"I don't know a thing." Her voice turned frantic.

"Don't worry," said John. "As soon as I know more, I'll give you another call. I promise."

"But—"

John cut her off, "I don't know anything else at the moment. I'll call you back."

He hung up—a bit more frazzled himself.

What now? If he called Stacey, he'd only upset her as well.

Damn-it! It's not like he had a real choice.

He picked up the phone and dialed.

. . . .

"Oh, my God, John! Was he serious?"

"As serious as I've ever seen him. He was muddied up and everything—supposedly from chasing Antonio out in the fields."

"What're we gonna do?"

"The only thing we can do right now is get to the bottom of things. I was thinking of talking to Jack as soon as they open."

"What about Antonio?"

"Don't worry. He'll get a hold of us."

"Let me get ready. I'll meet you there."

"How 'bout if I walk over to your place? I don't have a car."

"That's right. I'll swing by and pick you up."

CHAPTER 29

After a long, grueling trek along the riverbank, Antonio's stiffened body protested with a pounding headache. He felt the burning of his forehead as he clamped down on his jaw, refusing to follow the rhythm of his shivering shoulders.

His eyes sagged with fatigue.

The freezing cold had always been his worst enemy during Special Forces training. And even now, he could hear his PT officer barking at him: "Come on, Quintero! You wanted some action. Now put out. Come on! Come on!" Eventually, his fingers would begin contorting involuntarily from the elements, making it almost impossible to perform any task—so much that it almost caused him to drop out of training.

Now it alarmed him that his body might do just that—drop out.

The fog lights coming into view on the Rio Vista Bridge brought only bittersweet recognition. The red beacons, which provided warning to passing ships of pending collision, now called out to him as they cut through the heavy mist—helping to expose the first lift tower—while the rest of the bridge remained shrouded in fog.

He trudged forth in an effort to keep his blood flowing.

Once at the bridge, he scrambled to the pedestrian walkway, thankful for the absence of traffic and praying for it to remain that way. Otherwise, he might have to throw himself flat on the steel walkway or press himself to one of the steel trusses to avoid detection.

As he lumbered forth, the bridge gradually unveiled itself through the fog, while shrouding all that trailed in his wake, making it difficult to gauge any real progress.

Desperate for some rest, he leaned against the steel railing, but that only weighed him down further, underscoring the need to keep moving. When he turned to his right and to his left, both sides looked identical. It distressed him—and his frigorism only intensified the anguish.

Struggling to regain his equilibrium, he thought to look down at the river current to reestablish his bearings. Someone unfamiliar with the area might have remained disoriented. Fortunately, discipline and the will to survive had a way of clearing paths. He needed to press forth, holding on to the prospect of sanctuary. Father Flanagan had told him he could come by whenever he needed. At least, from what he remembered, those were his exact words, and a greater need than this hardly seemed imaginable.

The bridge continued to extend itself like an immense tunnel, with intermittent causeway lamps serving as guides. As he passed under them, they emanated a soothing warmth that urged him to stop and indulge; but that only meant putting off, if not compromising altogether, the one haven that awaited him.

Only once, when compelled by a passing vehicle, did he have to fall flat on the steel walkway. And the collapse made it virtually impossible to get back on his feet.

Each step further drained him of his depleting energy.

He found it harder and harder to distinguish between reality and delirium. At times he shook his head, thinking he had stopped, only to find that he was advancing the whole time. Then he looked around frantically to make sure no one had seen him.

His vision began to blur from the pounding in his head—so much that he questioned his first glimpse of St. Joseph's Parish. He turned around to verify his position. Sure enough, he found himself next to the municipal pool in Bruning Park—though he did not have the slightest idea how he got there. The last thing he remembered was trying to get through the bridge.

His struggle became like that of attempting to reach a restroom in time of great need. The closer one comes to it, the harder it gets to hold on.

He floundered his way around the church building, toward the rectory.

At least now he felt the safety of home. Even if he passed out halfway there, no one would find him until Father Flanagan walked out in the morning.

Suddenly, the rectory looked huge and intimidating, and his progress stopped.

He looked down and confirmed that his legs had collapsed.

He felt helpless.

Making one last appeal for God's strength, he forced himself up.

He tried to take a step forward, in spite of having no bodily sensation.

Strangely enough, he found himself getting closer to the rectory—almost as if someone were carrying him. He wanted to check his legs but knew to keep his focus on the rectory.

As long as he got there, it didn't matter.

Finally, leaning against the front door, he rang the doorbell.

After a spell, Father Flanagan answered.

Antonio tried to focus. "I need your help, Father."

"What happened?"

"It wasn't my fault."

"What happened?"

"You can't tell anyone I'm here. They're looking for me."

"Who?"

"The police."

. . . .

At that point Father Flanagan wrapped his arm around Antonio and helped carry him to his bedroom. He aided Antonio in removing his wet clothes and tucked him into bed.

Uncertain over whether to call John, Father Flanagan opted to wait until morning, when clearer heads would prevail. He paced his way to the living room, where he prayed through most of the night.

CHAPTER 30

At the crack of dawn, the vapid air gave the impression that the sun might refuse to rise any further. And even if it did, the invading clouds, which slowly consolidated the fog, would make sure that it remained hidden.

As this struggle for morning continued, John and Stacey parked in front of the police station and City Hall, the place where Main Street runs into the Sacramento River. Its current appeared especially strong and active, hauling within its rolling waves the spoils of dead tree branches, weeds of all sorts, and an occasional bellied-up catfish.

Within minutes, a light drizzle started coming down, dissipating the remaining fog.

"What time do you have?" said Stacey.

"Ten 'til."

Stacey pulled out a bottle of whisky from her glove compartment.

"What's up with *that*?" said John.

"It's just for emergencies."

"I don't think that's a good idea right now."

She took a swig anyway and put it back.

. . . .

Don came around the corner in his patrol vehicle, with windshield wipers on. He scarcely had time to shower and change into uniform before coming back on duty.

He tried to make up for his lack of sleep and an empty stomach with a cigarette.

What he did not need was a hostile group awaiting him.

He had scarcely stepped out of the vehicle when John and Stacey, now wrapped in raingear, accosted him from behind.

Don was not about to give them any satisfaction. As the sprinkle began to spot his pressed shirt, he hunched over into the vehicle, artificially poking around for his raincoat. He took his time, wallowing in every second that he put them off.

"All right," said Stacey, "what happened?"

Don remained hunched over. He felt no obligation to anyone. And with Jack behind bars, he figured Antonio's detention was just a matter of time.

137

He'd be damned if he let anyone spoil the moment.

"I have nothing to say," he said plainly.

"This is not a game, Don."

He came up with his raincoat in hand. "I'm not here to argue. We have an open case, and we're gonna pursue it to the end." He paused for effect. "That's all there is to it."

He mustered a surly grin and proceeded to the front door of the police station.

"You have no case," said Stacey.

Don turned around—truly amused—his shirt now blotched with rain. "Is *that* what you think?"

"What evidence could you possibly have?" said John.

"I can't disclose that. The case is under investigation, but I guarantee you, we have plenty."

"If he weren't your own nephew, I'd swear you did it yourself."

Don's face filled with revulsion. He grabbed his cigarette and threw it to the ground.

"What the hell are you saying?"

"Nothing," said John, taking a step back.

"Besides," Don tried to justify, "why would he be running if he wasn't guilty?"

"I don't know. That's what we came to find out."

Don smirked. "And how exactly do you plan on doing that?"

"We wanna talk to Jack."

"He's booked. He's not available for interviews."

"Why?"

"Because *we're* doing the investigation, not you."

"We wanna bail him out."

"Bail hasn't been set, so he's not eligible."

John scowled. "Why not?"

Don looked him over with fierce eyes. It usually intimidated, or at least calmed people down to a manageable level. "As long as Qüintero's out there, Jack's a liability, so there won't be any talk of bail, at least until the arraignment tomorrow afternoon." He smugly straightened his tie. "Unless Qüintero comes in voluntarily, of course."

A deafening screech suddenly came from around the corner.

Everyone turned.

Anne Smith's truck appeared, skidding almost out of control. Her small figure struggled to steady the steering wheel and maintain direction.

Everyone moved out of the way.

Her eyes projected an eerie determination that gave nobody confidence. She appeared to be heading straight for the building.

Don considered pulling out his gun.

She finally slammed the brakes, bringing the truck to a violent halt, next to the patrol vehicle.

"Hey!" said Don. "Whatta you think you're doin'? I could give you a ticket for that. You're gonna get someone killed."

Anne ranted out of the truck. "Screw you, Don! Where's my husband?"

"Where he needs to be."

"*Where* is he?"

"If you don't calm down, I'll throw you in there with him."

Stacey came up and took her by the hand.

"Whatta you gonna do?" said John. "Lock everybody up?"

Don gave him a pointed glare. "I'll do whatever I have to." He put on his jacket, not knowing how much longer he'd have to put up with everyone. Then he turned to Anne. "Jack's not available for bail. That's all there is to it."

He pulled out his keys and headed for the front door.

"Why not?" said Anne. "He hasn't done anything!"

"He aided the escape of a murder suspect."

"Damn-it, Don! Whatever happened must've been an accident. Besides, your nephew's no innocent bystander. Doesn't that come into play here?"

"That doesn't mean a damn thing."

"Why not? That should at least cast some doubt on your supposed evidence."

John stepped in. "You know she's right, Don."

Don's voice turned deep and severe. "Your boy lost, John. Why can't you just accept that?"

"I'll never accept that."

"Then you're just making life more difficult than it needs to be."

Stacey spoke up, "If you don't let us see Jack, I promise I'll formalize charges for this screwed up eye you gave me."

Don snickered. "You don't think the charges'll stick, do you?"

Stacey did not respond.

"Who's gonna believe you after two days?"

"Why not? I already reported the incident."

Don lost his smirk, and he looked over her eye patch. "You do whatever you want. But I guarantee you, it'll be scrutinized in light of your motive to defend Qüintero."

"That's good enough for me," said Stacey.

Don hesitated. "You do whatever *you* have to do. I'll do what *I* have to."

"If you do anything," said John, "anything at all, to harm Jack or Antonio, you're gonna have your hands full."

Don waved his hand boorishly. "Don't threaten me. Please."

"The hell with you too, Don."

"You know what your problem is, John? You're just—"

A honk came from around the corner.

All heads turned.

Officer McCabe's vehicle ran the stop sign as he made a right-hand turn and hastily approached the police station.

Once parked, he exited the vehicle with a concerned look on his face.

"I suppose you didn't find Qüintero," said Don.

"No," said McCabe. "I have some bad news."

Don frowned. "Is Barry still working at the farm?"

"Yeah, he's wrapping things up." He gave Don a questioning gaze. "I'm guessing you haven't heard."

"Heard what?"

"About your mom?"

Don felt a rock in his gut.

"What?"

"She's in the hospital. She had some kind of attack."

Don's face drooped. "What hospital?"

"Didn't you hear the call?

"No! What hospital?"

"Lodi Memorial."

"I'll come with you," said Stacey.

"No! I don't need you there."

"I'm going for your mom, not you."

"I said, 'no'!"

Don strode away before Stacey could say another word.

. . . .

Stacy stood her ground until Don drove off.

"I'm going to see her," said Stacey.

John gave her a cautious stare. "What about Don?"

"I'm not worried about him. I'll just wait 'til he leaves."

"Just be careful."

"Don't worry. Can you call in sick for me?"

"I'll call in for both of us."

She took his hand and squeezed hard, motioning with her eyes toward McCabe. Both John and Anne caught her drift, acknowledging with a smile.

Stacey drove off.

. . . .

They watched Stacey's car disappear down Front Street.

"Albert," said Anne, "can we see Jack for a moment."

"Sure."

He unlocked the front door and let them in.

CHAPTER 31

Sharon Lacey lay paralyzed in one of the critical care units of Lodi Memorial Hospital when Don walked in, his face pale and tired.

He glared at all the invasive instruments in Sharon's body. They made her look like a lab experiment. The intravenous catheters projected an anguish that cut through Don's core. They made him feel helpless. The beeping of the ECG echoed in his brain, as the oxygen mask fogged on and off with Sharon's labored breathing.

It all vexed him to the point of wanting to tear the instruments apart, one by one, as if blaming them for her current condition.

He took a deep breath—damning the sterile smell—as he walked up to her bedside.

Sharon's narrow face and sunken eyes made him question whether or not to wake her.

He reached out with a gentle hand to the shoulder.

"Hi, mom," he whispered

She struggled to open her eyes.

"It's okay, mom. Take your time."

As self-awareness set in, Sharon released a heartfelt sigh.

"How are you feeling?"

"Not so good, son," she muffled.

"What's wrong?"

"I'm dying."

"Please don't say that."

"Doctor said the nerve damage was extensive. They almost put me on a breathing machine. I'm lucky I can talk."

"He also said there's a chance you can recover."

"I can't stay around forever, son."

"Of course, you can—for a few more years, at least."

Sharon struggled to swallow.

"Even if I lived," she continued, "I wouldn't be good to anybody."

"What are you talking about?" Don asserted. "Dad needs you. We all need you."

"Your father won't be able to take care of me. I'd just be adding to his problems."

"And who's gonna take care of him?"

"That's *your* responsibility now—and your brother's."

Don pulled back at the idea. "*I* can't take care of him."

Sharon closed her eyes. A tear rolled out, and she began to cough.

Don quickly put his hand back on her shoulder. "I didn't mean it that way, mom."

The coughing slowly came under control. "Your father," She swallowed. "He doesn't have anyone else."

"But how am I supposed to take care of him?"

"I don't know. That's for you to figure out. Nothing else has brought you together. Maybe this will."

Don felt a pressure in his temples.

"No, mom! It won't work." He softened his tone. "You can't leave us."

They gazed into each other's eyes.

"Have you been praying?" asked Sharon.

Don frowned. "What for?"

"That might be the only thing that helps me get better."

Don had no response.

"What's the matter, son?"

"Nothing."

"What is it that's made you harden like this?" Her eyes welled up again. "I saw it happening to your father. Please don't let it happen to you. I couldn't bear it. Not now. Not when I'm getting ready to leave this world for good."

"Okay, mom! I'll pray. Just stop saying that."

"But you have to mean it."

"I do mean it." He cast his eyes to a far corner of the room. "I'll pray. I promise."

The words restored hope to Sharon's face.

"Is there anything I can get you, mom?"

"No, son. I'm fine."

"Anything you need from home?"

"No. Not really."

Don looked around the room.

"Where's dad?"

She did not respond.

"I said, where's dad?"

"He . . . didn't want to come to the hospital."

"Why? He should be here."

Sharon could not hold back the tears this time. "You should've seen him." She pouted. "He nearly collapsed with grief by the time the ambulance showed up at the house."

"Why isn't he here?" Don demanded.

"When the paramedic told him how bad I was, he just locked himself in the room. He hasn't even answered the doctor's calls. But I understand what he's going through. That's why you need to go see him."

"No! He needs *you*. You have to fight this, mom."

"I've fought so long already, son."

Don's throat constricted. "You can't give up!"

Sharon's tears continued to flow. "I've done all I can. It's up to you now."

"No! I won't let you."

"Then pray for me, son."

"I said I would."

"Yes. You did." She peered into his eyes. "I'll be praying for you, too."

A chill ran down his spine. "I don't need any prayers."

"We all need prayer, son."

"I don't need your damn prayers!"

Sharon closed her eyes. She could no longer hold back.

"Why did you do it, son?"

"Do what?"

"Take Mike with you. He was just a boy. You didn't have to take him."

A sweeping darkness brushed over Don, and his vision began to recede, as the previous night flashed before him—scene by scene. The fog. The bull. Mike yelling freakishly, waving his hands in the air before landing hard. Then complete silence.

As Don shook off the image, he stood befuddled before his mother. He beheld her like a frightened child, caught in his deceit.

He simply turned and fled.

CHAPTER 32

Stacey pounded her steering wheel in the parking lot of Lodi Memorial Hospital as Don finally marched out into the rain. And judging from the anguished look on his face, things were not good. She took the pint of whisky from her glove compartment and gave it two swigs before putting it back. As soon as Don drove off, she drifted out of her car and into the hospital.

Shaking off the rain, Stacey asked for directions and made her way to the critical care unit, where Sharon lay crying.

Stacey considered leaving, but Sharon noticed her almost immediately.

"Hi, honey," said Sharon, forcing a smile.

Stacey walked up to her bed and sat down. She put a hand on Sharon's cheek, then wiped her tears away. "It's okay, mom. You can cry. You need to let it out."

"What happened to your eye?" said Sharon, in response to the eye patch.

"Oh, just an accident. I'll be fine."

"But it looks so bad."

"Really, mom . . . it's nothing."

Sharon acknowledged with a nod. "Thank you for coming, dear."

"What's wrong?" said Stacey. "Why are you crying?"

Sharon gasped as Stacey caressed her cheek.

"What's wrong?" she asked again.

"So many things."

"Tell me."

"I'm not afraid to die, you know."

"I know," said Stacey.

"I just wish I'd lived long enough to see Craig reconciled to his children. I tried so hard to bring them together."

Stacey kept her emotions in check for Sharon's sake. "I know, mom. There's still hope."

"It's getting harder to breath, even with all this equipment. I know what's coming. I'm not going to fool myself."

"You can't do it all, mom. You have to trust that God will find a way to put the pieces together."

"Yes. I know. I just wish I'd seen it. That's all I wanted before I died."

Stacey felt her eyes welling up.

"I need your help, dear," said Sharon. "I need you to help me with something."

"What is it?"

"It's about Don."

Stacey lost her meager smile.

"There's no chance for you two anymore, is there?"

"No," said Stacey.

"I had a feeling." She closed her eyes.

"You know I tried."

"Yes, I know." Sharon looked at Stacey once again. "Can you at least try to help him? He needs a friend. He needs someone."

Stacey's head spun with conflicting emotion. She did not want to lie, but she didn't want to disappoint Sharon either.

Stacey reached under the sheets and took hold of Sharon's limp hand. "There's some things you need to know."

Sharon gasped. "I think I already know."

This caught Stacey by surprise. "About Antonio?"

"Yes."

Stacey tried to put her thoughts together. "I had no idea he was coming back."

Sharon sobbed quietly. "You don't have to explain, dear. You deserve your happiness, too."

"But I don't want it to affect you like this."

"No, dear. On the contrary, you brighten my day. I'm just sad for Don."

Stacey squeezed Sharon's hand. "Maybe I should let you get some rest."

"No, don't leave. I'm enjoying your company."

"But you need your rest."

Sharon projected a glow that Stacey knew full well. It was a love that could only be explained by the deep understanding they shared with one another—cultivated through years of struggle—which they could never share with anyone outside the family.

"I may never see you again," said Sharon.

"Mom—don't say that."

"I'm sorry, dear. I just feel so helpless."

"No," said Stacey. "You may be lots of things, but never helpless."

"Will you come visit me tomorrow?"

"Of course. I'll come every single day, while I can."

Sharon's crying stopped. "Thank you, honey."

"Just make sure you don't tell Don."

"Why?"

"Because he'll try to keep me from seeing you."

"Why would he do that?"

"Because he thinks you side with me too much. Maybe he's afraid I might turn you against him. I don't know."

"You might be right."

"The only problem is that I may have to leave town one of these days."

"Why?"

"Well, . . . there may be a superintendent position opening in Sacramento."

Sharon projected skepticism. "There's more to it than that, isn't there?"

"Not really."

"You've never lied to me, honey. Please don't start now."

Stacey fiddled with her hands. "It's just that . . . if Don finds out, he'll be sure to come after us, and you know that won't be good for anyone."

"You mean, you and Antonio?"

"Yes."

Sharon acknowledged with a blink of the eyes. "I guess I understand."

"He already made some threats."

"But you know he likes to talk."

Stacey felt she had already said too much. Then again, why not just tell her? It might be better than leaving her to speculate on her own. She would find out sooner or later, anyway. Better if she heard it directly from her.

"He's blaming Antonio for Mike's death," she said.

Sharon clenched her eyes, letting her head fall to the side. Her crying came out audibly.

"I'm sorry," said Stacey. "I just felt I should tell you. I didn't want to lie or give you any false hopes."

Sharon continued to sob. "That's okay, dear. I understand."

Stacey caressed Sharon's hand.

"There's some things I need to tell you as well." Sharon sniffled. "Now that it's starting to make sense."

"What is it?"

Sharon whimpered painfully now. "This isn't easy."

"Don't worry, mom. It's better if you rest. I can come back tomorrow."

"No!" said Sharon. "I have to tell you."

Stacey leaned over, with her cheek on Sharon's forehead, in an effort to calm her down.

The ECG responded with some quickening beeps.

"No, mom. This isn't good for you."

Sharon struggled to put her words together with long, hollow breaths. "Don . . ." she gasped impetuously.

Stacey tried to cuddle her. "It's okay. I'll come back tomorrow."

"No . . ."

The gasping became erratic—depriving her of breath.

Stacey released her, scuttling to the hallway, looking for assistance.

Within seconds, one of the nurses arrived. She checked the oxygen, while repositioning Sharon's bed to a more upright position.

"Everything's fine," she said, trying to calm Sharon down. "You're going to be alright."

Sharon continued to gasp.

At that point the nurse shuffled out.

She came back with a vial of Ativan, proceeding to syringe and administer a hefty dose through the intravenous catheter.

The nurse sat on the bed, with her fingers on Sharon's pulse.

As her breathing came under control, the ECG slowed its beeping.

"You're going to be fine," said the nurse. She looked up at Stacey. "It would be better if you let her rest now."

"No!" Sharon protested.

"Yes, Mrs. Lacey," insisted the nurse. "She'll be back tomorrow. You need your rest."

She nodded to Stacey that it was okay to leave.

Stacey said, "Thank you."

But she walked out conflicted.

CHAPTER 33

When Don returned to the police station, Officer Albert McCabe was still at his desk, finishing his report. That was one of the things Don liked about Albert. He did not like discrepancies, especially when they could come back and haunt the department.

"You almost done?" said Don.

"I've been waiting for you. How's your mom?"

Don had no particular desire to talk about the matter. "Not so good," he said.

"Sorry to hear that, chief."

"It must've been the news about Mike."

"Whatta you mean?"

"The reason for her attack."

McCabe frowned at the idea. "How could she've known?"

"One of the paramedics knows my brother Tim. I bet he went blabbing his mouth off." His forehead wrinkled with vexation. "It's all that damn Qüintero's fault."

"How can you be so sure?"

"You mean, besides all the evidence pointing to it?" He chose not to elaborate.

"We found tire tracks," said McCabe.

"What?" Don's brows narrowed. "Where?"

"Same place Quintero saw the car."

"And?"

McCabe gave him a blank look. "It corroborates his story."

"It corroborates the fact that someone *might've* been there. Nothing more. It could've been one of their own cars, for all we know."

"The evidence also supports the rest of his story—except for the rod wound on the bull. But even that could be true, for all we know."

"Are you buying into his story?"

"No. It's just that—"

"What?"

"Why . . . were you trying to erase the tire tracks?"

"Whatta you talking about?"

"I saw you sifting through the grass, trying to get rid of the tracks. They had your boot marks all over."

"What the hell you tryin' to say?"

"That it looks suspicious. That's all."

Don considered his words. "What does Barry have to say about this?"

"He thinks it was true . . . about the bull."

"Look, Al!" He was having a hard time being questioned. "This guy's guilty one way or another."

"How do you figure?"

"Worst-case scenario, he's guilty of involuntary manslaughter."

McCabe seemed to mull over the particulars with a wobbling of the head. "The other thing is that Anne and John wanted to bail out Jack."

Don scoffed. "So what the hell'd you do?"

"Don't worry. He's still there. But I have to admit, I was tempted to let him go."

"Look, Al. I don't give a damn what you think. Nobody does anything about this case without checking with me first. Is that understood?"

McCabe's brows narrowed. "You can't let it get personal, chief."

"It's *not* personal, damn-it! I'm just doing my job."

"What about the two gunshots you fired at him this morning?"

"I told you he's dangerous."

"He wasn't an immediate and personal threat."

"That's enough, Al. I don't wanna talk about this anymore." He marched past McCabe, to his office. "I'm tired of all this crap."

"Whatever you say, chief."

CHAPTER 34

John reluctantly called Stacey to help him pick up his car at the farm. Neither of them wanted to make the trip, but necessity compelled them.

They hardly spoke on the way there.

And walking through the scene of events only added to their somberness. At least they did not have to deal with Mike's body. Others had taken care of that, and the sprinkle had rinsed off most of the blood. They made sure to keep their visit short.

They were back at John's house by midday.

"Poor Sharon," said Stacey, as they walked in. "I wish I could see her again today."

"Just go first thing tomorrow."

John checked his answering machine for telephone messages. He had several, but the phone rang before he could listen to them.

"John. Finally! Where have you been?"

"Father Flanagan?"

"Yes."

"What a surprise. Have you heard about Mike Lacey?"

"Yes—regrettably."

"They're blaming Antonio."

"Is there any truth to the matter?"

"None that I can believe. We just got back from Jack's farm. It must've been an accident. There's no other explanation."

"Well, I'm glad to hear that. I have some news. There's someone here you may want to speak to."

"Speak to?"

"It's Antonio. He showed up early this morning—in very poor shape, I might add. He's still sleeping."

John turned to Stacey. "We'll be right over!"

. . . .

"So much for my follow-up with Maria today," said John.

"Don't worry. She'll understand."

"I'll make it up to her."

"I'm sure you will," said Stacey.

. . . .

Father Flanagan answered the doorbell. Rumors were already buzzing, and he was hoping to get some answers from John and Stacey. He offered them a seat in the living room, but they were too anxious to sit.

"I suppose you'd like to see him right away," said Father Flanagan.

"If that's possible," said John.

Father Flanagan walked them to the bedroom. They found Antonio sleeping and covered in sweat.

"Looks like he still needs some rest," said Father Flanagan.

John and Stacey agreed.

They returned to the living room and sat down.

John and Stacey explained to Father Flanagan everything they knew.

"Has Antonio had any contact with Don's mother?" asked Father Flanagan.

"No," said Stacey. "Why do you ask?"

"Well, one of the stranger rumors I heard this morning is that Antonio was also to blame for Sharon's condition?"

"That's bogus!" Stacey's eyes flared with anger. "I went to see her at the hospital this morning. If anything got her there, it's what happened to Mike. And that sure as heck isn't Antonio's fault."

Father Flanagan nodded. "Maybe that's what they meant."

"We can't mention this to Antonio," said Stacey. "It'll only upset him further."

"We have to be honest with him."

"But even Albert thinks it was accident."

"Then I don't see the harm in it."

"I think you're right," said John, "regardless of any uncertainties."

"Uncertainties?" said Father Flanagan. "Like what?"

"For one thing, nobody knows what Mike was doing at the farm," said Stacey. "Albert said they found some tire tracks where Antonio claimed to see a car drive off, after the accident, so John suggested that Albert interrogate Mike's Army buddies—the ones who were with him at Foster's the other night."

"Good. We'll have to see where that leads."

"The biggest threat I see," said John, "is that Don seems to be using Jack as leverage for Antonio to turn himself in."

"That's why I don't want to tell him too much," said Stacey. "He might just do it."

"What does Jack think?" said Father Flanagan.

"That he shouldn't even think about it," said John. "Jack was *there*—when they tried to arrest Antonio."

"But what could possibly happen?"

"They tried to shoot him, for God's sake."

Stacey tore off her eye patch. "You see this, Father? Don did this to me."

Father Flanagan frowned with displeasure. He almost felt attacked by Stacey, but he knew better than to take it personally.

"We're not about to take any chances," said John. "Jack figures that Anne and Rogelio can take care of the farm needs for now, and it shouldn't be more than a couple of days before Don's forced to release Jack, anyway."

"*If* they release him," said Father Flanagan.

"Well, at least Albert gave us his word to be fair about the investigation."

"You think he'll keep his word?"

"I don't see why not. It's Don I'm worried about."

Stacey began to squirm in her seat. "I'm gonna give my two-week notice at school. Then we can get the hell out of here." She caught herself. "Excuse me, Father."

Father Flanagan shook off the matter.

"We'll go to another state if necessary. No superintendent position is worth all this."

"You're right about that," said John.

"I can let Antonio stay here until things cool down," said Father Flanagan.

"Thank you, Father, but I think we need to get him out of here tonight. We can't afford to take any more chances."

"Just make sure you pray about this whole thing. You can't afford any mishaps."

"Oh, we will, Father. We will."

A reflective silence ensued.

"You think we should wake up Antonio now?" said Stacey.

"No," said Father Flanagan. "He should rest as much as possible. He needs it."

"But we need to talk to him."

"What's the rush? He'll wake up soon enough."

"I suppose."

"Look," said Father Flannagan, "I have to get back to some things, but you can stay as long as you need."

John and Stacey thanked him on his way out.

. . . .

Antonio walked into the living room with his eyes still swollen and the sweat freshly wiped from his face. He squinted at John and Stacey, while rubbing the remnants of pain from his temples.

"We were getting worried," said John.

Antonio sighed with a deep sense of shame. "You heard?"

"Jack told us everything."

"Where is he?"

"He wants us to get you out of here as soon as possible. He knows they'll have to let *him* go sooner or later."

"What about the farm?"

"He said it'll be fine with Anne and Rogelio."

Antonio frowned. "Where could I possibly go? I can't involve anyone else."

"Anne insisted on renting a motel for you—until we figure things out. It's just outside Sacramento. She said she'd come by and take you tonight."

"You think she'll be safe?"

"Should be. It's Stacey and me they'll be watching."

"I'm giving my two-week notice," said Stacey. "Then we can disappear for good."

Antonio bit down on his jaw. "I'm sorry about everything."

"It's not your fault. You didn't ask for any of this."

Antonio pressed his eyes with index finger and thumb. "After everything that's happened, I have to start questioning that."

"Don't start resigning yourself," said John. "Not now."

"We're gonna prove you're innocent," said Stacey. "Somehow or other."

"You think it'll make any difference?"

"Albert promised to be fair about the investigation. It'll make *some* difference."

Antonio thought over the options.

"I can't do it," he said.

"What are you talking about?" said Stacey.

"I can't just keep running. I don't wanna make things worse than they already are."

"How is leaving gonna make things worse?"

"I don't know, but they don't seem to have gotten any better since I left Mexico."

"It's the right thing to do, Antonio. Can't you see that?" Stacey reached out to him. "We're so close! Can't you feel it in your gut—that it's the right thing to do?"

"I'm not so sure."

"Putting yourself at Don's mercy isn't going to help any."

"Maybe not, but relying on gut feelings is no guarantee of anything, either. We can't assume that every gut twitch we have is the result of divine guidance."

"We've discussed the options," said Stacey, "and there's no other way."

Stacey's demeanor remained firm, yet vulnerable.

Antonio inhaled deeply. "Are you sure they'll let Jack go?"

"I'm sure of it," said John.

Antonio closed his eyes in frustration. "Fine. I don't wanna make things more difficult than necessary."

CHAPTER 35

A clear patch of sky opened up, and the shadows stretched well across the street by the time Don parked the patrol vehicle in front of his parents' house.

Glancing at the rearview mirror, he noticed his eyes remained red-rimmed and fatigued, while a familiar angst gripped his gut.

He pulled out a cigarette.

His dad never liked him smoking, so he lowered his window and puffed away, before deciding whether to approach the house. He grappled with what might possibly be keeping his dad from checking on his mom at the hospital.

He flicked his cigarette, annoyed at the lingering raw feelings about his mom.

Stepping out of the car, he leaned against the doorframe. He tried to catch a glimpse of indoor movement through the street-side windows.

With nothing coming into view, he forced himself across the street and up the porch stairs, only to find the front door bolted.

"Dad."

He knocked.

"Come on, dad. You have to talk to someone sooner or later."

No one answered.

With both hands, he blocked the sunlight on either side of his face, trying to catch a peep through the chiffon curtains, but nothing came into view. Nothing out of the ordinary, at least, except for the fact that his dad was nowhere in sight.

He clenched a fist and banged on the door this time.

"Damn-it, dad! I just wanna talk to you for a bit!"

Still, no one answered.

"Shit!" said Don.

He slammed the door once again, stomping about with clenched fists at his waist. Why the hell did everything have to be so complicated? The sight of one of his mom's flowerpots prompted an abrupt kick that sent it flying over the porch railing.

It crashed to pieces on the concrete driveway.

Annoyed by his own conviction, he tromped back to the car.

He slumped over and contemplated the house, wondering once again what the hell could possibly be going through his dad's mind.

He could never tell. And it looked like he wouldn't find out any time soon.

As he turned the ignition key, a flicker of memory suddenly brought him to attention.

The house key in the back yard—it might still be there!

With renewed expectation, he hopped out of the car, this time walking up the driveway, along the side of the house, past the broken flowerpot.

Ever since he could remember, that key had been there—for emergencies—in case he or his brother got locked out.

As the back yard came into view, behind his dad's truck, he came to a sudden standstill.

He found it hard to process the overgrowth of weeds before him.

He couldn't believe it. He'd never seen it so filthy.

It didn't make any sense.

Even if his dad couldn't take care of it anymore, it wasn't like he couldn't afford a gardener. It wasn't even that much work. He and his brother had been responsible for keeping the yard clean when they lived at the house.

Once he stepped through the gate, the grass reached up to his waist. The only thing taller was the barren apricot tree, which itself looked like it hadn't been pruned in years. No wonder they hadn't given him any apricots lately. Only some hibernating flower bulbs, which his mom must have planted along the perimeter of the house, kept the weeds at bay.

He cut a path through the overgrowth, heading toward the crawl space vent that lay next to the patio entrance. Pushing the weeds aside, he exposed the red-tinted wire that held the key in place on the inside.

Grabbing the vent from both ends, it took some effort to loosen, but it eventually slid out with a sprinkle of debris.

As he surveyed the vent hole, a waft of stale grime struck his face.

To his shock, the crawl space revealed a considerable termite infestation. He better tell his dad before it compromised the foundation.

He proceeded to untwist the wire and remove the key from the vent.

Feeling triumphant, he wondered how his dad would react when he saw him. Surely, he wouldn't expect him to remember the emergency key.

He opened the patio door and made his way through the laundry room.

"Dad."

He went through the kitchen and found a vacant living room.

Disappointed, he headed to the back room.

"Come on, dad. Where are you?"

He returned to the living room and noticed one of the lamps had been toppled over. That must've been where his mom collapsed.

He shook off the image and headed upstairs.

"Dad."

The house remained silent.

He couldn't remember the last time he experienced this much quiet in his dad's house.

Suddenly, his mind overwhelmed him with unwelcome thoughts of foul play. What if someone had broken into the house? And what if his dad—

He impulsively grabbed for his gun.

Holding it close to his body with both hands, he warily made his way up the stairs.

Finding the master bedroom closed, he reached for the doorknob with one hand and threw it open, recoiling back against the wall.

At the lack of sound or movement, he lurched, pointing his gun through the door at a sharp angle. With nothing coming into view, he jumped to the other side and did the same.

For a second, he held his posture—coming to terms with the scene before him.

He gradually lowered his gun and stood upright.

His dad lay chest-down on the bed—sleeping—one hand hanging over the edge.

Don holstered his gun and went to shake him by the shoulder. "Dad."

He didn't respond.

"Damn-it, dad. Why don't you just cut it out?"

He shook him again—harder this time.

The rigormortic resistance hit Don like a lightning bolt.

He clenched his teeth.

There was a bright flash as the blood drained from his head.

His knees buckled as he reached for support. He tried to resist, but a back spasm finished toppling him onto the bed, next to his dad.

The room seemed to spin, almost as if trying to flip him off the bed.

And fighting it only made things worse.

Feeling the immense weight of his limbs, he made one last audible exertion, but it came out as nothing more than a wheezy, broken strand of sound: "D—"

Chapter 36

When Don regained consciousness, he attempted to pick himself up slowly, but the room refused to stop spinning. He closed his eyes, with his head still pulsating, spiraling him deeper and deeper into a fathomless pit. It continued spinning, until the nauseous build-up of bile drove his body to convulsions—forcing him to crawl to the bathroom, where he finally found some relief—spewing all but his guts into the toilet.

He just hung there, pining for relief.

Worn out, and without the slightest concept of time, he remained sprawled over the toilet, until the heaving subsided, waiting to regain his equilibrium.

In due course he hauled himself back to the room.

He braced his arms on the bed and gazed over his dad's petrified body. He found it easier to manage this time, though no less painful.

His muscles remained taut and aching.

He closed his eyes, only to grapple with memories that now remained mired in the past.

With a rub of the face, he tried to expunge as much as possible. How the hell was he supposed to manage this in light of his mom?

He growled under his breath, before hoisting one arm and slamming the bed with his fist.

Unwary—at the core of his anger—a splintered sense of pity for his dad suddenly took hold.

The notion shook him, leaving him unsure of how to respond.

He eased himself onto the bed.

Only inches away, he considered the being that now lay inert and beyond grasp.

He reached out, almost against his will, lured by a lurking void in his soul, until he found himself caressing the back of his dad's head.

But he quickly put a check on his emotions.

After a spell, he picked up the phone and called the coroner.

CHAPTER 37

The doorbell startled Antonio. He sat in the living room, reading C. S. Lewis' *The Problem of Pain* from Father Flanagan's library. He glanced at the clock on the wall. His duffel bag was ready—John had brought it for him—but he wasn't expecting Anne until at least nine in the evening. It was barely past six.

Father Flanagan came from the kitchen and answered the door.

"Hi, Father." It was Officer McCabe. "Forgive me for interrupting your evening, but I'm guessing you know why I'm here."

Father Flanagan almost choked—throwing a glance behind the door at Antonio.

Antonio stared back from the recliner.

As McCabe waited for a response, Father Flanagan's eyes jumped from Antonio to McCabe, then back to Antonio.

"I'm here," said Antonio.

With a sudden shuffle, McCabe side-stepped into the rectory, behind Father Flanagan. His hand remained over his pistol as he cleared a path to Antonio.

When their eyes locked, McCabe scanned Antonio for indications of sudden movement.

Once satisfied, McCabe straightened up, but he kept his hand over his pistol.

"I'm sorry for having to do this," he said, "but it'd be easier if you came in voluntarily this time."

Antonio nodded. "Stacey said you promised to be fair about the investigation."

"And I intend to keep that promise. All I need is for you to cooperate."

Antonio got to his feet with both hands behind his head. "What about Jack?"

"Don't worry about him. I'll let him go as soon as we get there."

McCabe approached cautiously. He took hold of Antonio's left arm and cuffed it.

Father Flanagan observed at a distance.

"How'd you know I was here?"

"John and Stacey should've come to visit you separately." McCabe secured both arms behind Antonio's back. "That made it very suspicious."

"You won't do anything to them, will you?"

"Not if you cooperate."

"I'll cooperate," said Antonio. "Did you find out who drove Mike to the farm?"

"No. We talked to his Army buddies, but they knew nothing about it. They were pretty shocked about the whole thing."

McCabe walked Antonio out the front door, into the gnawing gust, to his patrol vehicle.

Father Flanagan remained quiet.

"Can you let John and Stacey know where I am, Father?"

"Of course."

Antonio turned to McCabe. "Do I stand a chance?"

McCabe guided him by the arm. "I think you'll be fine. Based on the evidence—worst case scenario—I think you're looking at manslaughter. But I'm not even sure that'll stick."

Antonio sighed. "So why isn't Don here?"

"His dad just passed away."

Antonio stopped in his tracks. "What?"

"From what I understand, he called the coroner no more than an hour ago."

"What happened?"

"I really don't know. The main reason I'm here is so he won't be tempted to do something crazy in his state of mind. He doesn't even know I found you yet."

Antonio thought over the implications. "You think he'll be satisfied with simply finding me?"

"Don't worry. There's not much he can do once you're in jail."

"Nothing has stopped him so far."

"You'll be fine. Don't worry."

Antonio found it easier not to look back at Father Flanagan as McCabe led him to the patrol vehicle.

Chapter 38

After leaving the morgue, Don drove straight to the hospital to see his mom. He didn't know what he'd say or how he'd feel, but he needed to see her. He couldn't tell her what happened, but he could at least spend time with her. Anything to help her feel better. Anything to help himself feel better. She'd find out what happened soon enough, anyway.

In the meantime, he took it out on a cigarette, wondering if his brother Tim had gone to see her. Tim had always been closer to her—ever since he could remember.

. . . .

Sharon was still awake when he arrived. Even in good spirits. And although the medical equipment remained attached, it seemed to get lost in the background this time. If she was still in pain, she didn't show it—smiling behind her oxygen mask at the sight of him.

"You're back."

Her gaze seemed to pass right through him, as if her focus were off, coming to rest at a point just behind him. It gave him an eerie feeling—almost as if he weren't there.

As long as she didn't mention Mike, everything would be fine.

"You're looking better," he said.

"Thanks to you."

Don frowned. "What's that supposed to mean?"

"That I'm happy to see you."

"You tryin' to make me feel guilty?"

"Guilty? About what?"

He regretted the question. "Nothing, mom."

He studied her face. Part of him wanted to thank her for looking better, but the notion struck him as silly.

It continued to bother him that he could not get their eyes to meet.

"Is something bothering you?" said Sharon.

"Yes," he found himself saying.

"What's the matter?"

He tried to sidestep the question, but only exposed himself further. "Have you ever wished you could change something?"

"Many times," she said. "Why? What's wrong?"

"I don't know."

Sharon gave him her full attention. "What is it?"

"I'm not sure."

"Not sure about what?"

"About being a cop anymore," he spurted.

She looked at him in disbelief.

"I'm just getting tired of it," he said. "Maybe running for mayor isn't such a bad idea after all."

Sharon's eyes widened. "You can't tell Don that. You'll just get him upset."

Don scowled at her in confusion. "What are you talking about, mom?"

"That it's not fair to Don, just because you don't want him to be a cop."

"Mom, what are you saying? It's me. I'm the one talking to you."

Sharon blinked repeatedly.

"Mom, it's Don," he repeated. "I came to see how you were doing."

"Don? Where?"

Don took her by the hand. "Here, mom. It's me."

"Don?"

"Yes. What's wrong?"

"What are *you* doing here?"

"I came to see how you were doing."

"I'm fine," she said. Then she smiled anew. "Your father came to see me."

Don tried to lock eyes with her. "What?"

"You should've seen him. I've never seen him so full of hope."

"What are you talking about?"

"Your father. It looks like my getting sick helped him realize a lot of things."

Don found it hard to respond. He leaned against her bed, holding her hand, as he came to rest on his knees.

"When?" he said. "When did you see him?"

"Just a little while ago. Didn't you come with him?"

"No."

"I thought you did."

Don remained confused.

"You're not still mad at him, are you?" she asked.

Don swallowed hard this time. "No."

"I'm so happy," she said. "He said he was taking me home real soon."

"That's crazy," Don protested.

The glow in Sharon's eyes receded. "You *are* still mad at him, aren't you?"

"No!" he said—out of desperation, more than anything.

"Then why are you getting upset?"

"I'm not upset. I just don't understand what you're saying."

"It's true, son. I've never seen your father so well. It's enough to make me happy that I got sick. He said he'd take care of me when I got home."

"You have to get better, mom. You can't go on deluding yourself like this."

"What're you talking about?"

"Dad couldn't have come to see you. You're confused."

"No," she said. "I'm not confused. Why are you still mad at him?"

"I'm not mad!"

"Then why are you acting like this?"

"Like what?"

"I don't know. Like you're resentful, or something."

"I'm not resentful."

"Then what is it?"

Don sighed with resignation. "I don't know, mom."

She looked at him with longing in her eyes. "I love you, son."

"I know, mom."

"You father loves you too," she said. "He told me."

He suddenly let go of her hand and stood up. "I have to go, mom."

"Why?"

"I just have to go."

"But I'm telling you about your father. Isn't that more important?"

There was no response.

"Isn't it?" she pleaded.

"Yes, mom."

"Then why do you have to leave?"

"Just get better, mom. I'll do whatever you want. Just get better."

Chapter 39

Once John and Stacey arrived at the rectory, they insisted that Father Flanagan repeat the whole story. Everything—from the beginning—as if to convince themselves that they were not imagining things. That he was not making things up.

Their blood boiled as Father Flanagan repeated the details.

"How could we have been so stupid?" Stacey's eyes teared with anger.

"There's no sense in regrets," said John, trying to be practical. "We need to figure out what to do from here."

"But how could they have seen us?"

"That doesn't matter, as long as we can still count on Albert."

"And what if we can't?"

"We can't worry about that until it happens."

"The hell with that! I'm not waiting for anything." She mumbled something to herself. "I know where Don keeps an extra set of keys to the police station. I could bust him out, and they'd never know what happened."

"No," said Father Flanagan. "We need to think this out clearly. Otherwise, things'll get out of control—the very thing Antonio wanted to avoid."

"He's right," said John. "Whatever we do, we need to do it right."

Stacey's eyes faded behind her withering glare. "Nothing else is gonna work."

"We'll have to let God be the judge of that," said Father Flanagan.

"That's right," said John. "I don't want you to end up in jail with him. Maybe it's better if we sleep on it. There's nothing we can do for now, anyway."

Stacey's face hardened. "You expect me to be able to sleep?"

John took a breath of defeat.

"We need to take care of this *now*," she insisted. "And I can do it with or without you."

"I don't think any of us expects to sleep," said John, "but we need to think hard about what to do next. We can't afford for things to get worse."

Stacey gave him a long and hard stare. "I need a damn drink."

167

A sudden knock came from the front door.

John and Stacey turned to Father Flanagan.

"Who is it?" he said

"It's us, Father."

"Jack and Anne!" said Stacey.

Father Flanagan welcomed them in.

"What happened?" said Stacey.

"They wouldn't let us talk to Antonio," said Anne.

Jack nodded. "They let me out before I could see 'im."

"We need your input," said John. "Whatta you think we should do?"

"I wanna see him," said Stacey. The stubborn flare in her eyes refused to yield.

"Ya might as well forget it," said Jack, trying to be as sympathetic as possible. He turned to John. "All I know is what I told ya last time. They mean business. Or at least Don does. He'll do whatever it takes ta make sure Antonio's convicted."

"You think we can trust Albert?" said John.

"I don't trust any of them. But Albert's not the problem. Whatever Don decides ta do, I don't think Albert'll be able ta help— whether he wants to or not."

"Did Don say anything while you were there?"

"He tried ta get whatever he could outta me."

"Did you tell him anything?"

"Of course not." He smiled. "Except to throw 'im off here and there."

"What did he say?"

"Hell, the only thing that kept 'im from kickin' the crap outta me was knowin' he wouldn't get away with it."

"So what're we gonna do?" said Stacey.

"I don't know what else we *can* do, except hope the judge'll let 'im out on bail. Then again, I'm sure Don'll do everything he can ta make sure that doesn't happen."

"Then I'm gonna bust him out."

"I thought we decided that wasn't an option," said John.

"How do you plan on bustin' 'im out?" said Jack.

"She doesn't. It's just some crazy idea she got in her head."

"It's possible," said Stacey, "and you know it."

"You could end up in state prison," said Jack.

"That's what I'm trying to tell her," said John. "It's not worth it."

"I'll leave the country if I have to."

John turned to everyone for support.

"Anne," he said, "can you please help me knock some sense into her?"

"It's true," said Anne. "We need to wait for the arraignment. See what Don does and take it from there."

John nodded in agreement. "And if there's anything we can do to help with Albert's investigation, let's do it."

Jack slapped a fist into the palm of his hand. "That's it!" he said. "We can investigate this thing ourselves, while we look for a lawyer? It all happened at the farm, anyway."

Everyone turned to Jack.

"That is an idea," said John.

"We can document everything, especially where Don tried ta get rid o' the tire tracks. And a friend of mine knows the district attorney. If we get a hold of 'im—I mean if Don tries ta pull any surprises—we'll be ready for 'im."

"Sounds like a plan," said Anne. "Whatta you think, Stacey?"

Stacey looked half convinced. "I guess it's better than doing nothing."

"I think it's a great idea," said John. "When do we start?"

"As soon as there's enough light."

"We'll have to call in sick again, but we'll be there for sure."

"I can meet you guys there," said Stacey. "I need to see Sharon first thing in the morning."

Everyone agreed.

CHAPTER 40

On the way back from the hospital, Don puffed on his cigarette, wondering where to take his mom after her discharge from the hospital. His brother Tim was out of the question. He could hardly help himself at the moment. But with his dad gone and his mom's delusions, he could no longer conceive of putting her in a nursing home. The only remaining option was his guestroom, even if he had to pay someone to take care of her. He'd have to look into it later.

For the moment he had no desire to return home to an empty house. He wanted to forget as much as possible, and keeping busy at work was the best way to do it.

He would sleep there if necessary.

He'd done it before. Might as well stick with what worked.

When he walked through the back door of the police station, he was glad to find it empty. Nobody to tell or ask him anything.

He walked into his office and leaned back in his chair—eyes closed and hands folded over his chest. He took a deep breath, still feeling the ache in his bones.

Forget work.

Maybe he could catch up on some sleep.

After his nap, he could—

. . . .

Next thing he knew, he was exploring the depths of a vaguely familiar cave. As he examined the sharp and rugged contours of its walls, he rediscovered that they could cut flesh through mere contact. He did all he could to keep his distance, only to be frustrated by some equally-sharp, protruding stalagmites.

A lack of visual depth gave him a sense that the surrounding walls were closing in on him, as a whirling gust of wind whistled through.

It spoke to the core of his bones: "Get out! Get out now!"

The elemental onslaught brought him to a sudden standstill, and with no sense of direction, a frenzied panic ensued.

He gawked, searching for any means of escape.

With darkness looming in every direction, only the wind-flow gestured of possibilities.

170

He trotted in the direction of its source, hoping to outpace his growing claustrophobia.

The terrain remained unrelenting in its threat.

Thankfully, a spark of light in the distance renewed his hope.

He kept his pace.

As he approached, the light swelled suspiciously—with no natural source of illumination—prompting him to proceed with caution.

The cavern opened up to a self-illumed treasure trove, at what appeared to be the heart of the cave. The treasure covered an entire wall and spilled into some of the cavern's extending veins. Gold, pearls, gems—everything he could imagine. Piles and piles of them.

He stared with pounding heart and covetous eyes.

No breeze remained.

He forgot about leaving and lost himself in lustful passion.

Yet an imperceptible menace kept him from reaching out to the treasure. Muffled echoes made it clear that he was not alone. Whatever the source, it seemed to be watching and ready to safeguard the treasure. A beast within the shadows of the cave.

Now and then, it gave shrouded glimpses of its enormous horns and crimson eyes.

For a moment he thought he could smell its stale breath.

Stricken again with panic and the urge to escape, he refused to leave without the treasure.

Without losing sight of the threat, he mustered the courage to break some rocks off the cave wall, lacerating his hands in the process. When he looked, he saw blood rolling down his arms, but he hardened his face and licked up the blood.

Then, more annoyed than anything, he hurled the rocks at the beast.

In a flash, the shadows moved and the beast lunged—exposing itself as an enormous, black bull.

In desperation, Don turned and ran.

He sprinted down a passageway.

Then another.

And another.

Suddenly, he found himself running across the living room of his parent's house, dodging cluttered piles of junk and shabby furniture. When he turned to take another look at the beast, he found that it was only his dad chasing after him. And there was nothing menacing about him. He looked as normal as ever.

He decided to stop and chat with him.

And the more he approached, the more pleasant became the appearance of his dad.

When he stood next to him, his dad moved his lips as if to speak. Without warning, his mouth opened grotesquely—trying to swallow him whole.

As he fought him off, a violent earthquake shook the house, cracking the walls and bringing it down to its foundation.

. . . .

Don jerked himself awake. He was sweating.

He sat up with both hands on his desk, looking around to make sure no one had seen him.

He remembered the dream. All of it.

It took a moment for him to shake it off.

As he reached for a bottle of water, he caught sight of a FAX he didn't recognize. He must have overlooked it when he came in.

He picked it up and read.

An initial confusion slowly morphed into a fiendish smile.

He gloated over the letterhead; but the handwritten note at the bottom gave him even greater reason to relish. It looked like Officer Miller's handwriting: "He's in the holding cell. Albert found him at the church rectory."

He looked up from his desk, overcome with a desire to jump and shout.

Forgetting everything, he paraded over to the holding cell.

Chapter 41

Still awake, when the steel door screeched open, Antonio looked up from the bunk bed—not the least bit surprised to see his late-night visitor standing in the dim light.

Antonio tried to project a stoic exterior.

"Looks like your plan failed miserably," said Don.

"What plan is that?"

"To take Stacey away from me."

Antonio turned away with a distaste in his mouth. "There was no plan, Don."

"I guess it doesn't really matter now. We'll just have to let the Mexican authorities judge for themselves."

Antonio looked up, as Don waved the FAX in front of him. "I just got a FAX from INTERPOL. It would appear that we weren't the only one's looking for you. Seems like you've been keeping busy elsewhere." He held the FAX up for Antonio to appreciate. "Does Stacey know of your extra-curricular activities in seminary?"

"I told her everything."

"Really?"

"It was an accident."

"Then there should be no problem."

"Concerning what?"

"I've been wondering what to do once we found you. Now it seems that my dilemma's been resolved. We're gonna have to ship you back to pay your dues in Mexico. Unfortunately, John and Stacey won't be able to help you there."

Antonio's eyes remained on Don.

"Oh, don't worry," said Don. "It happens to the best of us."

Antonio shook his head. "I have to admit, you've been quite the challenge for me."

"Really!" Don beamed with delight. "Tell me about it. I'm all ears."

"I know we're supposed to love without reserve, but when I think of *you*, I need to pray for the very will to do so."

"What the hell makes you think I need your love?"

"We need all the love we can get. To think otherwise is to delude ourselves."

"Why would you care?"

Antonio shrugged. "If God cares, then *we* need to care."

"Pleeease! Save your sermons for someone else."

"We're human, Don. That makes us social creatures. We need one another, whether we admit it or not. I know I'm not what I could be, but God's still working on me. He's working on all of us—all the time. The one thing I know is that God makes no mistakes. And as much as I don't like myself at times, I also know that God created us with a special purpose in mind. But unless we let Him work *in* us, it'll never materialize."

Don turned to walk away. "I said what I needed to say. I didn't come to hear sap stories."

"Stacey once told me," Antonio deepened his voice, "that, in light of your divorce, not having children was the best thing that could've happened."

Don jerked himself around. "*That* is none of your business?"

"I'm not so sure that she was right."

"What the hell would you know?"

"Maybe if you had children, God could've touched you more deeply and saved your marriage." He tried to anticipate Don's thoughts. "It's all part of faith, you know. If you never risk anything, you'll probably never receive anything in return."

"You still expect me to believe your bullcrap in light of this FAX?"

"I told you it was an accident."

"So whatta you expect me to do? Let you go?"

"Of course not."

"Besides," said Don, "having kids didn't do a damn thing for my dad. And it sure hasn't helped my mom."

"Nobody's perfect, Don. We're all spiritually crippled—in one way or another. It's something we need to work through. It just takes a lot of effort and pain to overcome. Precisely the kind your mom has had to endure."

"Then why isn't *she* happy?"

"If I had to guess, I'd say she felt alone. Stacey tells me that she shares in your pain, but you haven't been willing to help her through her pain. It takes real courage, you know—precisely the kind that most of us avoid in our desperate pursuit of happiness. The sad thing is that by avoiding the struggle, we hinder the growth and character that make a deeper joy possible. We're too selfish and shortsighted."

"Then why aren't you happy?"

"I already told you I have my share of problems. Problems never go away. What I do have is a fundamental peace that not even you or my problems can steal away from me."

Don snickered. "And how's that gonna help you now."

"You know I didn't do it."

"All the evidence points to you."

"Is that why I saw another car drive away after it happened?"

Don's eyes narrowed.

"That was you, wasn't it?"

"Screw you, Antonio!"

"I didn't do it, and you know it." Antonio held his gaze. "You don't have to do this, Don. You're not just hurting me. You're hurting yourself."

Don almost laughed. "Don't give me this psychological bullcrap. In case you haven't noticed, you're the one that's locked up."

"These bars don't mean a thing when you know who's guilty."

"Oh, please!" Don gave the cocky smile of one who understands more than others might think. "I know how much you hate me."

"No," said Antonio. "That's not entirely true."

"Maybe just a little?" Don mocked. "Isn't that supposed to be against your principles? Or maybe you don't have any, after all. Is that why you left seminary? You get tired of not being yourself and doing what you really wanted? To—"

"*No!*" Antonio broke in. "I admit my faults, but I never made it a point to make anyone's life difficult."

Don placed his hand over his chest. "I . . . am . . . so touched."

Antonio closed his eyes, wrestling with frustration. He took a deep breath. "Why are you so full of spite?"

"Whatever, Qüintero." Don gestured his baton in front of him. "Maybe it's for the same reason you are. What the hell gives you the right to come back and screw with people's lives? Especially my wife. Everything was fine before you came."

"No, Don. Everything was not fine. Some of this may be my fault, but you have to acknowledge your share of it."

"You can rot in here for all I care."

"Well, it looks like you might get your wish this time."

Don's lips curled. He turned before another word could be said, storming out of the cell and slamming the steel door behind him.

CHAPTER 42

Early the next morning, Stacey walked into Sharon's hospital room and found her sleeping. The tension in her face had lifted. And her breathing, although slow, remained calm under the oxygen mask.

Stacey sat at Sharon's bedside, absorbing the peace that radiated from her. With the back of her hand, she reached out and tapped Sharon's forehead.

After some time, Stacey began to pray—whispering an occasional thought.

"Everyone's been thinking about you, mom. We have great plans for when you get out of here. Did I tell you—"

Just then, Sharon's nurse walked into the room.

Stacey looked up. "She looks better today."

The nurse checked Sharon's pulse. "Unfortunately, it's not as good as it looks." She considered her next words. "There's been a complication."

Stacey sulked. "What kind of complication?"

"She went into a coma last night."

Stacey lost her composure, swinging her gaze over to Sharon. "Is she gonna be okay?"

"It doesn't look promising."

"What're her chances?"

"I'm afraid it's just a matter of time."

Stacey observed Sharon's meager breaths. They appeared weaker, upon closer inspection.

"She did leave something for you," said the nurse.

Stacey gave her perplexed, but full attention. "For me?"

"Your name is Stacey, isn't it?"

"Yes."

The nurse flipped through Sharon's medical chart, pulling out a folded piece of paper.

"The swing shift nurse left a message that we should give this to you." She handed the note to Stacey. "She helped her write it. It's supposed to be important."

Stacey flicked it open.

It read: "It was Don who took Mike to the farm."

The initial shock brought a constricting pressure to her chest. And the ensuing disorientation drained her face of color, with a sudden elevation in heart rate.

"Are you okay?" said the nurse.

"Yes. Thank you," said Stacey, trying to compose herself. "Did she say anything else, by any chance?"

"That's all I know. She said you'd understand."

"Yes, I understand."

"Are you sure you're okay?"

"I'm sure."

Stacey reached for Sharon's hand—to console herself as much as Sharon—but the anger continued to flare inside of her.

She grabbed her eye patch and tore it off, once and for all.

Before heading out, she turned to the nurse. "Would you mind giving me that nurse's phone number? It's terribly important."

CHAPTER 43

Having spotted Don's vehicle outside the police station, Stacey burst through the front door. She marched past Officer McCabe's desk, nearly knocking over one of the office clerks. All eyes turned in her direction—taking special note of her exposed, purple eye—as she barged into Don's office and slammed the door behind her.

Don looked up from his phone.

The exaggerated display enthralled him—until he recognized the stubborn expression on her face.

"I'll have to call you back," he said, hanging up with a sneer. "Whatta *you* want? You here to beg for Qüintero's release?"

Stacey glared at him with confidence. "I'm here to let you know that I found out who took Mike to the farm."

Don considered her words. "Really?"

"Yes, really."

"And how would you have found that out?"

"Let's just say I heard it from a reliable source."

She pulled out Sharon's note and threw it on the desk.

Don looked at it with cold speculation. "Where the hell'd you get that?"

"I told you—a reliable source."

"According to who?"

"Your mom."

"My mom?" His brows furrowed. "What are you talkin' about? She can barely speak."

"One of the nurses relayed the message to me."

He took another look at the note. "And you expect me to take this seriously?"

"I can't imagine why you wouldn't."

"She's not in her full senses, for one thing."

Stacey slapped Don's desk with the palm of her hand. Her lips thinned with anger. "Just because she can't move, doesn't mean she can't think!" She kept her eyes on him. "I'm sick of you treating her like this. She doesn't deserve it."

Don glanced at the blind-covered windows of his office.

"Either you lower your damn voice—" He pointed his finger at the door. "Or you can get the hell outta here!"

Stacey pointed at her bruised eye. "You see this!" Her eyes opened wide. "You see this! You're not gonna shut me up anymore."

"Look—"

"Never again! You hear me!"

Don leaped out of his chair, lunging forward, to take hold of her.

She pulled back, as Don's thighs jammed into his desk, hampering his sudden reach.

"You better get outta here," he said, "before I have someone drag you out."

"Why don't you do it yourself?"

There was no response.

"You afraid of what it might look like?"

"Andrew!" Don called for one of the officers.

"Still worried about that reputation, I see."

"Andrew!"

"I talked to the nurse who took the message from your mom."

Officer Andrew Duarte poked his head through the office door. "What's going on, chief?"

"I want you to escort her outta here immediately."

"She's willing to testify," said Stacey.

"I don't give a damn," said Don. "There's nothing here about the specific incident. Besides, my mom's delusional right now. Whatever she said wouldn't be admissible in court."

"What makes you think she's delusional?"

"She thinks she spoke to my dad yesterday."

Stacey gave him a blank look.

"My dad's dead," he said. "And he never went to see her at the hospital. She imagined the whole thing."

Stacey remained silent.

Don waved for Officer Duarte to come into the office.

"By the way," said Don, "I thought you might wanna know that Qüintero's name came up on the INTERPOL wanted list." He searched Stacey's face for signs of vulnerability. "That's right. It seems that his criminal activity finally caught up with him." He concocted a sinister smile. "You didn't fall for that seminary crap, did you?"

"Go to hell, Don."

"I thought we'd have to prosecute him ourselves, but someone seems to have volunteered for us. Nothing like saving some taxpayer money, huh?"

The loathing welled up inside Stacey. "Not that you care," she said, "but why don't you visit your mom, instead of wasting your time on what's only gonna make you more miserable?"

"I'll see her when I'm ready."

"That might be too late."

He turned to Officer Duarte. "I think we're done. Why don't you get her outta here."

"I just came from seeing her," said Stacey.

"I told you to leave her alone."

"And I told you you'd have to kill me first."

"Get her outta here!" said Don, throwing out his arms for emphasis.

Officer Duarte pulled the door open. "I'm sorry," he said, taking her by the arm.

"You better get things in order with her," said Stacey. "She's in a coma."

Don fixed his eyes on her.

"It's true," she said.

Don remained silent.

"Go see for yourself."

"Why wouldn't they have told me by now?"

"They probably tried. Maybe you just haven't listened to your messages. If you weren't so worried about Antonio, you'd probably know by now."

CHAPTER 44

The morning chill cut through John's bones as he drove into Jack Smith's farm. He and Anne were already at work in and around the tractor shop—taking pictures and notes—determined not to let their lack of effort be a deciding factor.

They waved to one another as John slowed to a tentative stop.

He forced himself out of the car and into the morning numbness, which drove him straight to the cover of the shop. Might as well get a glimpse of the bull.

As it turned out it remained well-preserved. Hopefully, the pictures would stir controversy over why Don felt the need to shoot it.

Outside, the shoe prints and tire marks remained discernible.

Together, they coordinated. They gathered. Measured. Drew. Conjectured. Leaving nothing to chance. They made good headway, at least until about nine-thirty, when they could no longer ignore Stacey's absence.

"I don't like this," said John.

"There's gotta be a reason," said Jack.

"That's what I'm worried about."

"Whatta ya mean?"

"I think I might know where she is."

"Then give 'er a call. Tell 'er ta get her butt over here. I know she's worried, but if she wants Antonio out, she needs ta help."

John agreed. He went to the phone inside the shop.

No one answered.

He dialed her office as well.

Still—no answer.

He went back outside.

"I think I know where she might be." He headed in the direction of his car. "I'll be right back."

"You gotta be kiddin'," said Jack. "It can't be that serious."

"You think something happened to her?" said Anne.

"I'm not taking any chances."

"Just hurry back," said Jack. "It's supposed ta rain later. That could wash away what little evidence is left. It was bad enough with yesterday's sprinkle."

"I'll be back."

CHAPTER 45

A wave of clouds drifted in from the west as Stacey drove into the sadly familiar cul-de-sac. She parked as far into the back corner of the driveway as possible, taking another swig of whisky before exiting the car. She looked around, hoping no one had seen her, before turning toward the cover of the bougainvillea vine that arched over the entrance to Don's house.

She fumbled through her purse for the house key.

Time was of the essence. For all she knew, Don could change his mind about seeing his mom and show up at any moment.

She bolted through the door and closed it behind her, securing the chain lock for extra protection—or at least as a warning—if Don came back.

A quick scan of the living room revealed dirty clothes piled on the couch, the remote control nearby, and a couple of empty TV dinners on the coffee table. Not a surprise with no one to help look after things.

She tried to tell herself that Don deserved it, but it seemed so pointless now.

She'd fare much better by staying focused.

Still, she couldn't help but wonder where she'd be if Antonio hadn't come back?

Probably not any worse. Though definitely not any better.

If she had to choose, she'd take the good with the bad any time. No point in a static existence.

She thought about it on her way up the stairs.

Definitely no point in a static existence. After all she'd been through, an inert life meant no life at all. She had to make it count—whatever was left of it—and the only person to make it count with was Antonio.

She smiled.

Nonetheless, as she entered the master bedroom, her eyes filled with tears.

She couldn't help it. Regret overtook her.

She took a deep breath and pursed her lips. How could she still feel sorry for herself? Everything was going to be fine. It had to. That's why she was there—to accomplish her mission and get the hell out.

Any distraction could spell the difference between success and failure.

She walked over to the chiffonier and opened the top drawer. Shoving Don's t-shirts to the side, she dug all the way to the bottom.

There! In the corner. The keys to the police station.

Next to them lay Don's pistol, still in its holster. The one she trained with—in case anyone ever broke into the house.

She picked it up, rolling it in her hands like a piece of jewelry. She pulled it out of the holster and felt its cold surface. Without slipping her finger to the trigger, she closed one eye and aimed at one object, then another.

When a picture of Don suddenly crossed her view, she dropped her aim.

Suddenly, a clicking noise from downstairs gripped her.

She turned and listened.

It came again—louder this time.

It had to be the chain lock on the front door.

She jammed the gun back in its holster and threw it in the drawer.

With keys in hand, she slammed it shut.

The downstairs noise ceased, but if it was Don, he'd be wondering what was going on, especially with her car parked outside.

As she shuffled down the stairs, she considered her escape plan. If she went out the front door, he might still be there. If she ran out the back and over the fence, she'd be stranded without her car. And if he caught her—

She whipped around the newel post, heading for the back door, when a silhouette passed one of the side windows, heading for the back yard.

With a lump in her stomach, she spun around and shot back to the front door.

She yanked on the nob. Damn-it! She forgot about the chain lock.

As she unlatched it and flew out the door, she heard a shuffle in the side yard doubling back in her direction.

She couldn't reach her car fast enough.

"Hey!" she heard.

She stumbled into the car and turned on the ignition.

"Hey!" she heard again.

She put the car in reverse, looking up for the first time, as a body lunged at the car. And she was about to step on the gas, when recognition finally set in.

First the clothes.

Then the face.

She didn't know what to make of it.

"John?" She lowered her window. "What're you doing here?"

Her heart pounded.

"I should be asking you that," he said, almost out of breath. "What happened to your eye patch?"

"I can't talk here."

"Where, then?"

"Anywhere but here."

"Why don't you leave your car at the apartment? We can take my car to Jack's farm from there?"

"Sure. I'll see you there."

She backed out of the driveway and sped off.

Chapter 46

Stacey parked at her apartment complex and jumped into John's passenger seat.

"So what were you doing at the house?" said John.

"You don't need to get involved," said Stacey.

"It's a little too late for that. I caught you in the act, remember?"

She did not respond.

"Did you find the keys to the police station?"

"Yes."

"Are you gonna use them?"

"Yes."

"Damn-it, Stacey! Do you really know what you're doing?"

"I thought about it all night."

"What about our investigation?"

"It's not gonna make a difference."

"Don't you think it's at least worth a try?"

"I thought it was—until I spoke to Don this morning."

John frowned. "Why are you wasting your energy?"

"I wasn't planning to. But when I went to see his mom this morning, I found her in a coma." John winced. "Of course, I wasn't able to talk to her, but she left me a message." She tried to anticipate John's reaction. "It *was* Don who took Mike to the farm. That was the message she left with the nurse."

John grimaced, with a shake of his head. "What did Don say?"

"That it didn't matter anymore."

"How could it not matter?"

"He said Antonio's name came up on the INTERPOL wanted list."

John's face went blank. "Was he serious?"

"He said they were gonna send him back to Mexico. If they do, there won't be a thing we can do to help."

John tightened his grip on the steering wheel. "When did you plan on doing it?"

"Tonight."

"Have you thought it all out?"

"Pretty much. I'll just create a distraction. Once everyone leaves the station, everything should be easy."

"What if someone shows up while you're inside?"

"I'll improvise."

"It's too risky."

"I'll have to take my chances. There's no other way."

"I can watch the door for you," said John.

Stacey frowned. "There's no point in putting both of us at risk."

"Well, I'm not gonna let you do it alone. It's less of a risk with both of us. In fact, it's probably better if *you* watch the door—in case someone shows up. They'd probably be less suspicious if they saw you, instead of me. Just play it off. Tell them you need to talk to Don or something. I'll go in and let Antonio out myself."

Stacey considered the details. She took a deep breath and exhaled with force.

When the smell of liquor hit John, he straightened up in his seat.

"What the hell!" he said. "Have you been drinking?"

Stacey's thoughts wavered. "Just a couple of drinks."

"It's ten in the morning, for crying out loud."

"I was just nervous about going into the house, that's all."

John scrutinized her.

"It's no big deal," she insisted.

"No big deal? We need clear heads to pull this off."

"I know. I know. Don't worry."

A prolonged and awkward silence ensued.

"I'm sorry," said John, finally. "But you know I'm just trying to help."

"I know," said Stacey. "I promise I'll stop."

She grasped John's right hand from the steering wheel. That calmed them both.

"The other thing," said John, "is that you better have everything—and I mean everything—ready to leave on a spur-of-the-moment. Because once you leave, there's no coming back."

She squeezed his hand. "Thank you."

John cleared his throat and nodded, without taking his eyes off the road. They were past the bridge and well on their way to the farm.

Meanwhile, the clouds continued to intensify.

"And we can't let Jack and Anne get the slightest suspicion of what's going on," said John. "The less they know, the better. Otherwise, we jeopardize everything."

"I understand."

"I'm sure they'd like to help, but we can't involve them any more than we have already."

"Don't worry. I'll do everything I can to help right now. As long as they see some enthusiasm, they shouldn't suspect a thing."

"Good," said John. "That's good."

Chapter 47

Don had to inhale deeply from his last cigarette before he could gather the courage to go up to the hospital room and see his mom. He hadn't verified the suitability of the guest bedroom at his house, but if Stacey was correct, it would have to do.

He began to pray on his way up.

He didn't even catch himself until he was almost there. Then he just felt silly. He couldn't remember the last time he had prayed. It irritated him, actually. The last thing he wanted was his mom's sentimentality. As far as he was concerned, it never did a damn thing for her.

His presumption shattered as he walked into the chaotic scene of doctors and nurses scrambling about, with the ECG beeping irregularly in the background.

"She's still not breathing," said one of the nurses.

"Is the ventilator functioning?"

"Yes."

"Give her another dose of epinephrine."

Don stood stiff and open-mouthed.

"Is she reacting?" said the doctor.

"No."

One of the nurses came up to Don and took him by the arm. "I'm sorry, sir, but you're gonna have to wait outside."

"I'm her son," he protested.

"I'm sorry, sir, but you're gonna have to wait outside."

The nurse escorted him out as he looked over his shoulder.

"Is she gonna be okay?"

"We're doing everything we can."

She left him outside and returned immediately.

As he looked back from the hall, his hands began to shake. There had to be something he could do. Anything! He hated feeling helpless.

Yet the only thing that came to mind was "pray."

But what damn difference would that make?

He gripped his eyes shut.

"What the hell do you want from me?" he found himself saying, with his fist to the ceiling.

He leaned back against the wall, sliding down to a squatted position.

He began to weep.

Next thing he knew, he felt as if something like a warm blanket had fallen over him.

"Don't go, mom," he mumbled, no longer conscious of his surroundings. "Please don't leave us."

. . . .

A few minutes later, Don stood to his feet, as the doctor came out of the room.

"How is she?"

"We managed to stabilize her."

Don had to rough his throat. "Is she gonna be okay?"

"She's in critical condition. We had to put her on a ventilator."

"Can I see her?"

"I highly recommend it. Just make sure you don't give her any bad news. She can't afford any of that right now."

Don gave him a dumb look.

"I understand your father passed away last night," said the doctor.

"Yes, but I thought she was in a coma."

"Oh, she is. Don't get me wrong. But in most cases patients can still hear and understand everything you say."

Don continued to look puzzled. "She sounded pretty confused when I came to see her yesterday."

"Well, you never know with these things."

Don nodded.

"We've done as much as we can. The only thing you can do now is pray."

Don questioned him with elevated eyebrows.

"Unless you don't believe in that stuff," said the doctor.

"Does it make any difference?"

The doctor grinned. "Well, I can't deny what I've seen."

"You mean miracles?"

"Sometimes."

"How do you know it's not coincidence?"

The doctor reflected. "I suppose that's possible."

"Then how can you be sure?"

He put a hand on Don's shoulder. "As long as the coincidences keep happening, I'll just have to keep believing."

He excused himself.

"What if nothing happens?" said Don.

"There's always that possibility."

. . . .

Don took his time getting back to the room.

One of the nurses remained behind, checking the dilation in his mom's eyes.

The ventilator remained painfully intact, while the intravenous catheters maintained her electrolyte and blood pressure level.

It horrified him—that she might be slowly slipping away.

He vowed not to move from her side this time.

He'd sit with her as long as it took.

Pulling up close, he whispered into her ear, "I'm sorry, mom. You were right about dad. He did need you. He needed all of us."

He sniffled and wiped his nose, waiting for the nurse to leave the room.

"I need you too," he continued. "Please don't go. I'll just sit here and pray with you."

He took her by the hand.

Chapter 48

With all the evidence on their side, Jack and Anne celebrated their cataloged findings, while John and Stacey did their best to play the part. As long as no one suspected them of ulterior motives, all would be fine.

After some final congratulations, everyone departed in good spirits.

John and Stacey rehashed their plans on the drive home.

The clouds remained thick and heavy. With any luck, they hoped the rain would keep everyone inside, reducing the possibility of witnesses.

Upon arrival, Stacey hastened John into her apartment.

"You sure everything's packed?" said John.

"Everything I'm taking, yes. I already double-checked. Just make sure you don't lose the key to the apartment."

"Not a chance."

"And make sure you bring Antonio's bag."

"Of course. I have nothing else to remember."

"Good. As soon as it gets dark, we'll start taking my things out slowly."

"You wanna go over the plan again," said John.

"Not really."

"We're only gonna get one chance."

"I've got it, John. I couldn't forget if I wanted to."

"Well, after I get Antonio out, just give us enough time to get to the church. We'll be waiting for you there. And pull all the way to the back. I'll throw Antonio in, and you'll be on your way."

"And you—don't forget the gloves once you're inside. I don't wanna see your face on the news. I couldn't bear it."

"Don't worry. I'll be fine."

She took him by the hand. "You promise?"

"I promise."

"And you *are* gonna call Maria, right?"

"I told you I would."

"I really like her, John. I want you to be happy."

"As long as you and Antonio are fine, I'll be happy."

"No, John. I mean really happy—for yourself, not just for us."

"I know."

"Good. 'Cause we'll be thinking of you."

"Just make sure you write Antonio's brother when you think it's safe. He'll make sure I get the message."

"Of course."

CHAPTER 49

Don gave into the nicotine anxiety, stepping out to the hospital courtyard, where the clouds had turned dark grey—heavy and suffocating under their bloated weight. He didn't want to drive anywhere, so he looked for someone to bum a cigarette off of. Besides, his brother Tim hadn't arrived, and he needed to stay close to his mom.

He lit up and puffed quickly, while the distended clouds began to unload their pressure on the world below. He knew what was coming with his mom. He even accepted it. He just didn't want to think about it, so he welcomed any distracting thoughts that came his way.

"Yes, mom," he said to himself.

A quick breeze shot through the courtyard.

"Yes, mom." He hesitated this time. "I can do that, too."

When he finished his cigarette, he headed back upstairs.

. . . .

Don found the nurse caring for his mom.

"I'm glad you're back," she said.

He looked over at his mom. "What's wrong?"

"She's still deteriorating."

He ground his teeth, wondering why the hell Tim hadn't arrived.

"You need to decide what to do, Mr. Lacey. Her blood pressure's not getting any better."

"Have you seen my brother?"

"No."

He didn't want to make the decision alone, yet putting things off might only prolong her suffering.

"Can we just let her body decide for itself?" he found himself saying.

The nurse put a light palm on his shoulder. "Of course."

She checked the IVs once again, before leaving.

"If you need anything," she said, "anything at all, just come and get me. I'll be making my rounds."

"Thank you," said Don.

He pulled a chair up to his mom's bedside and held her hand.

"It's okay, mom. It's me."

He could hardly feel her pulse.

"You can rest now," he continued. "Don't worry about me. I'll do my best to take care of things."

His eyes welled up. "I know you're tired. No one can blame you."

As he spoke, a flood of memories flashed before him.

"I'll just sit here and pray with you."

He tightened the grip on her hand.

"Is that okay, mom?"

CHAPTER 50

Don cried like never before as the rain pelted his car on the way home. And with the wipers thrashing his windshield, he could hardly see through the thick of the night.

He was tired. That's all he knew.

Really tired.

He needed to rest before he went completely mad.

The skies thundered above.

Two parents gone in two days. What the hell could God be up to? It was more than anybody should be expected to handle.

"Okay!" he yelled. "You got my attention. Now what?"

He wiped his heavy eyes.

"I want an answer!" he sobbed.

After all that happened, he figured he deserved an answer.

Maybe—with Antonio out of the way—he could at least work things out with Stacey.

It would please his mom. He knew that much.

. . . .

After calling 9-1-1 from a local pay phone and reporting a multi-suspect break-in at the bank, Stacey sped over to the police station, where she confirmed that the vehicle of the officer on-site had temporarily left the premises.

She parked in the Hap's Bait parking lot at the corner, across the street from the police station, where the rain provided some cover and she could keep track of the traffic. She glanced at her watch. She figured John should be reaching the back door of the station any second.

From her vantage point, she hoped to keep track of his progress as well.

In the midst of the adrenaline rush, she reached for the whisky bottle in the glove compartment. Thankfully, her nervous shake helped her catch herself, and she pulled her hand back.

She had to stay focused.

That's when she saw John crossing the street.

. . . .

Feeling like a secret agent, John had broken into a sweat under a double layer of jackets and a hood dripping with rain. As he looked up, he found it hard to believe his first glimpse of the back entrance to the police station.

He felt butterflies in his stomach. Only two doors stood between him and Antonio.

With a quick glance to the rear, he moved forward with anticipation.

In no time at all, Stacey and Antonio would be on their way—happy at last—with no one to stop them, just as they deserved.

The sound of tires swooshing through the street brought him back to attention.

He turned and saw car lights coming down the street.

When he hopped onto the sidewalk, his legs almost cramped.

He grunted and gave each leg a shake.

Fortunately, the car veered off in a different direction.

. . . .

Don rubbed his face as he stepped out of the car, making a run for the front door of his house. He could almost feel the welcoming, soft covers of his bed as he shook off the rain and wiped his shoes on the door mat.

When he slipped his key into the doorknob, it turned without effort.

Intuitively, he looked up and tried the deadbolt.

It was also unlocked.

He looked out into the rain, scanning for anything suspicious.

He pulled out his gun—just in case—as he entered the house.

Finding nothing behind the front door, he listened for noise.

The drumming of the rain made it difficult.

He shuffled into the kitchen and family room with his pistol ready, occasionally looking behind, to make sure no one snuck out the front door. If someone was there, he'd find them.

He quickly scanned the garage before heading upstairs.

The silence remained troubling.

He checked the master bedroom, then the guest and junk room, including the closets.

Nothing appeared stolen.

He hustled downstairs and checked the rear door. It remained locked. He opened it, looking out into the yard.

Nothing but rain.

He locked it and went to do the same with the front door.

For all he knew, in his current state of mind, he could have left it unlocked. Who would want to rip off the police chief, anyway? It didn't make sense.

A bit more at ease he started unbuttoning his shirt and made his way up the stairs.

Fatigue quickly reasserted itself, making his bed look more and more inviting.

As he bent over to untie his shoes, he spotted a picture frame lying on the floor. It had obviously fallen from the chest of drawers.

Annoyed, more than anything, he reached for his pistol once again.

It couldn't have fallen on its own. With the windows closed and no breeze, someone must have knocked it over.

He picked up the frame and put it in its proper place.

That's when he noticed the top drawer had been left ajar.

Don's brows narrowed as he took another scan of the room.

Everything appeared in place.

As he questioned his sanity, a sudden grip in the gut reminded him of the gun.

Alarmed at the potential threat, he yanked open the drawer.

But the gun was there.

He checked the bullets.

Also there.

Then a shiver cascaded down his bones.

He fumbled through the t-shirts—shaking each one before throwing it out—looking for the extra set of keys.

Who the hell could've taken them?

No one knew they were there.

His eyes opened wide—except for Stacey!

He threw the pistol back in the drawer and ran downstairs, charging out the front door.

. . . .

After opening the back door to the police station, John shook off the rain in triumph and slipped on some shoe covers to avoid leaving tracks.

His heart pounded so hard it caused him concern.

What if he keeled over? Wouldn't that be a sight?

He shook off the image and walked past some filing cabinets, heading straight for the cell door.

. . . .

Stacey picked at her fingernails. She hadn't seen any activity for several minutes. What the hell could John be doing? Every second counted. She felt like jumping out of the car and checking for herself.

. . . .

Antonio woke up to the rattling of the cell lock. Another late-night visit, he figured. He squinted and stretched, trying to defog his brain.

When the door opened, he looked up and stared.

"Let's go," said John.

Antonio hesitated—unconvinced.

"Let's go!"

"What're you doing here?"

"I'm getting you out, that's what."

"How'd you get in?"

"It doesn't matter. Let's go."

Antonio jumped off the bed. "You can't do this. They'll throw you in jail."

"I said, 'Let's go.' Nobody's gonna find out."

"No," said Antonio. "I'm not gonna be responsible for you going to jail."

"The only way I'm going to jail is if you don't move *now*."

"I can't keep running!"

John's face cringed. "You're running from injustice, for God's sake. What's wrong with that?"

"There's nowhere else to go. I've got to face this sooner or later."

"Stacey's waiting for you as we speak. She's ready to leave. Everything's packed."

"Where? Where is she?"

"She's waiting at the church."

Antonio found it hard to make sense of things. "What about her job?"

John grabbed Antonio by the sleeve. "She doesn't want you sent back to Mexico. Isn't that more important?"

Antonio held his ground. "What about you?"

"If we leave now, nobody finds out. If we don't, we're both in trouble."

. . . .

With the wind picking up and skies thundering, Stacey found it hard to believe deliverance could be so close at hand. She ran nervous fingers through her hair as a rush of blood rekindled a slight throb around her bruised eye.

She breathed deeply. Peace remained elusive for her until they reached complete safety.

In the meantime, she questioned how much more she could take.

Suddenly, Don's patrol vehicle came into view—speeding in her direction.

Her heart pounded as she mechanically reached for the glove compartment and gulped down two swigs of whisky.

Don zoomed by without noticing her car, coming to a sliding halt in front of the station. He jumped out into the rain.

Without hesitation, Stacey threw open her car door and yelled out to him. "Don!"

He jerked around—already soaked under the rain.

His crazed look shook her. But with so much at stake, she had no choice but to follow through—at least long enough for John and Antonio to get to the church.

. . . .

John took off his top-layered jacket and handed it to Antonio—to protect him from the rain and conceal his identity on their way to the church.

Antonio slipped it on as they headed out the back door, holding the tip of his hood to prevent it from flying off.

John led the way, trampling through puddles and runoff.

About a block from the station, they crossed Front Street and headed up to the church.

. . . .

Stacey stepped out of the car, and into the rain, as Don splashed his way towards her.

She braced herself.

"I've been waiting for you," she declared.

He beamed at her with wet, bulging eyes as he came up and took her by the throat.

"I want those damn keys right now."

She almost swung back at him.

"What keys?" she squealed.

"The ones you took to bust out Qüintero."

He searched her pockets with his free hand.

"I don't know what you're talking about."

"Where the hell did you put 'em?"

He threw her to the side and went to search the car. "Don't screw with me, damn-it! Nobody else could've taken them."

Stacey zipped up her jacket, praying that he wouldn't force her to open the luggage-filled trunk and expose the entire plan.

"You're not gonna find anything," she said.

Don drew back from the car.

"Then what are you doing here?"

"I told you. I was waiting for you."

"Waiting for what?"

"I need to talk to you."

He shook his head. "Why here?"

"I checked the house, but you were gone."

He scowled, almost in confusion. "So what do you want?"

She thought carefully. "I want you to let him go."

He glared at her—then broke out in laughter.

"Maybe we should talk about this inside." He pointed to the station as the rain rolled down his face.

"No." Her face flushed. "I just wanna know if you'll let him go."

"Well, why don't you come in, and we can talk about it?"

"I can't. I've gotta go."

His brows narrowed. "Do you wanna talk, or not?"

"I just wanna know if you'll let him go."

He gave her a crooked stare. "No. I won't. And you knew that."

She nodded nervously.

"Then why did you come?"

She remained silent.

"*Why* did you come?"

He studied her face—before casting a gaze to the police station.

She grabbed him by the arm; but he yanked himself loose and scurried to the station.

"Wait!" said Stacey.

She hastened after him.

The skies thundered as Don sorted through his keys to open the front door.

"Don't do anything to him," said Stacey, trying to maintain the facade.

He turned to her. "Why shouldn't I? He's ruined everything I have."

She had nothing to say in response.

He went back to unlocking the door. "You wanna say good-bye before we ship him back to Mexico?"

"No." Her eyes widened.

"No?" He looked her up and down. "What are you so worried about?"

"Nothing."

He took her by the arm. "You shouldn't be so worried."

"I'm not worried."

He opened the door, tugging her behind him.

She pulled back.

"What the hell's the matter?" said Don. "Don't you wanna see him?"

"Let *go* of me!"

"I thought you wanted to see him."

"No!" she said, yanking herself lose and running back to her car.

· · · · · · · · · · · · · · ·

Dripping in rain, Antonio and John reached the back of the church.

"Where's Stacey?" said Antonio.

"She's supposed to be here. Give her a minute."

. . . .

Don fumbled through his keys and opened the holding cell.

He couldn't believe his eyes.

How did she get him out? And where the hell was he?

He push-kicked the cell door. It swung back in defiance.

Why was she still hanging around? It didn't make any sense.

He whipped around, determined to get some answers.

By the time he ran out into the rain, she was coming out of the parking lot.

"Stop the damn car!" he roared.

She barely heard him through the drumming of the rain, looking out her driver-side window. It was obvious she had no intention of stopping.

He chased after her, pulling out his gun and pointing at her tire.

. . . .

The thundering discharge gripped John and Antonio to attention.

"That was a gunshot!" said Antonio.

John felt the ricochet down his spine. "It was thunder."

"It was a gunshot," Antonio insisted.

"It couldn't have been."

Antonio jerked a glance at him. "Whatta you mean, 'it couldn't have been'?"

They heard it again.

"I'll go check," said John in a quivering voice.

Antonio held him back. "It could be dangerous."

John stared back with vacant eyes. "Someone could be hurt."

Antonio read his anguish. "What's wrong?"

John didn't respond.

"What's wrong?"

John remained silent.

"Where's Stacey?" said Antonio.

"I told you. She'll be here any minute."

"Where's she coming from?"

"Her apartment, I guess."

Antonio frowned. "You guess?"

"She's coming from her apartment."

"How do you know?"

"Because that's how we planned it."

"Planned what?"

He didn't respond.

"Don't lie to me, John."

"She's supposed to be here any second."

"Where's she coming from?"

"Her apartment."

"That gunshot came from the police station."

"I'll go check."

"I'm coming with you."

"You can't!" said John. "You have to wait for Stacey."

"Someone could be hurt." Antonio dashed through the rain, in the direction of the police station, before John could say another word.

"If someone sees you, it's all over!"

John kicked the ground and chased after him.

. . . .

Don continued his chase as Stacey's car slowed down, veering off to the side of the street. He couldn't see anything through the shattered rear window, so he ran toward the driver's side door, wondering if she passed out.

The car ran up the sidewalk and hit the stop sign before he could reach her.

Don stopped.

Then he approached slowly—afraid to look inside.

. . . .

Antonio ran like a freight train down Main Street, as John shouted far behind, and the scene began to reveal itself—through the downpour—up ahead.

. . . .

By the time Don looked inside the car, Stacey lay over the passenger seat, with blood gushing out the back of her neck.

With heart pounding, his eyes welled up.

He dropped his gun.

"Why?" he whimpered.

Stacey's lips moved ineffectually.

"Don't move," Don pleaded. "I'll call the ambulance."

As he stepped back into the rain, her body went limp.

He froze.

. . . .

The storm continued to pelt the scene as Antonio's mind went into overdrive at the sight of Stacey's car crashed into the stop sign and a shattered rear window.

His sloshing presence prompted Don to reach for his handgun.

He turned with a pathetic glare.

"What happened?" said Antonio

"You killed her."

Something like an electric shock pierced Antonio's chest. When he took another step, Don raised his gun.

"Stay back," he said.

"I just wanna see her."

"You aren't seein' shit." Don fired at Antonio's thigh.

Antonio clenched his eyes at the pain that shot throughout his leg; and the sudden weight of his body rolled him onto the flowing runoff.

"How does that feel?" said Don. "Not so good, huh?"

Antonio looked up with a grimaced face and an exhaling grunt.

Don gloated.

Undeterred, Antonio braced his arms, trying to pull himself up to Stacey's driver-side window. He needed to see her—no matter the cost.

Don raised his gun and shot at his feet, knocking him off balance and onto the ground.

"I said, stay away from her!"

As the downpour penetrated Antonio's open wound, he rolled over in mounting pain.

"That's where you belong," said Don. "Groveling."

Antonio braced his bleeding leg.

"And this one's for coming back in the first place," said Don.

He pointed his pistol.

. . . .

"No!" yelled John, panting his way across Front Street.

But it was too late.

The shot echoed in all directions.

. . . .

Don turned his aim on John.

John raised his arms and approached cautiously, as Antonio lay sopped, with blood streaming in all directions.

He gazed at Stacey's shattered, rear window.

Suddenly, the sound of sirens came from down the street.

"Get the hell away!" said Don.

John stood his ground. "Can't you see what you've done? You need help, you demented bastard."

Don fired a warning shot at John's feet.

John flinched, but he refused to back down.

"I said, get away!"

"I'm not going anywhere," said John.

The siren stopped as the patrol vehicle came into view, with emergency lights still flashing. It came to a sudden halt in the middle of the scene.

Officer McCabe jumped out in full raingear.

Don, soaked to the core, continued to point his gun at John.

"What's goin' on, chief?"

"This doesn't concern you, Al. Why don't you get outta here."

"I'm sorry, chief. I can't do that."

"I said, get the hell outta here!"

McCabe lifted an open hand, hoping to reason. "Put down the gun, chief. Everything'll be just fine."

"No," said Don. "Nothing's gonna be fine—ever again."

He took the gun and aimed it at his head.

McCabe lost his composure. "What the hell you doin', chief?"

"Finishing what I started."

"That's not the way to do it."

"It's the only way left."
Don closed his eyes and fired.

CHAPTER 51

When John tried to see Antonio at the hospital, the authorities would not allow him. Only immediate family members, they told him. He had to rely on Rubén for updates. But that worked out fine. John and Rubén had lots to catch up on.

John's son, Gary, flew in for Stacey's funeral; and even though he returned to D.C. after only a few days, he began to call more regularly to keep tabs on John.

Meanwhile, after a thorough investigation, Officer McCabe concluded that Don had led the charge on acting irresponsibly. And having done a poor job of shooting himself, he would likely be serving serious time after he got out of the hospital and went to trial.

In the interest of justice, McCabe cleared John as much as possible, recommending a probation that would allow him back to work.

John preferred a leave of absence.

. . . .

Not until the rescinding of the INTERPOL notice did the authorities grant general access to Antonio. Then John showed up in typical fashion—with book in hand—hoping to keep Antonio's mind occupied.

"*The Consolation of Philosophy*?" said Antonio with raised eyebrow. "Are you serious?"

"They told me you were feeling better."

"Not enough for Boethius."

John welcomed the banter.

Antonio sat up, exposing the bandage on his upper chest. It had healed well. However, the sudden constriction on his repaired femur prompted a cringing groan.

"Take it easy," said John.

Antonio massaged the pain perimeter around his cast. "I'll be fine," he said. "They had to do reconstructive surgery."

"Rubén told me."

John helped Antonio adjust his bed to a more upright position.

"Anything new from the outside world?"

"Not really." John handed Antonio the book, hoping to distract from the impact of his next comment. "I'm sorry you had to miss Stacey's funeral."

Without saying a word, Antonio leafed through the book's oxidized pages.

"Have you thought about what you're gonna do?" said John.

"Not sure yet."

"You can stay with me as long as you want."

"I know, John. And you know how much I appreciate that."

They drifted into a moment of reflection.

"So what happened with INTERPOL?" John prompted. "First, they were sending you to Mexico? Then, all of a sudden, they were letting you go."

"They found out the truth." Antonio set the book aside. "I didn't do it."

"You wanna share some specifics?"

"From what I understood, the foremen on the neighboring farm weren't so much in agreement, after all. They ended up fighting amongst themselves, and someone else got seriously injured. That's how they got to the bottom of things."

"Does that mean you're going back to seminary?"

"I don't know."

Antonio reached for the book again. He studied the table of contents, as if trying to remember its teaching.

One of the nurses came in to take his vitals. "You're doing great," she said. "If you keep this up, we're gonna have to send you home in a day or two."

Antonio thanked her on the way out.

"That's good news," said John.

Antonio took his time in answering. "I still can't make sense of what happened."

John empathized in silence.

"If it's any consolation," he said, finally, "neither can I. And I've tried. Believe me."

"I've questioned all my motives," said Antonio. "All my actions. And I still can't make sense of it. I just wanted what was best—even as things got complicated."

"That's just the way it is sometimes."

Antonio's tone deepened. "I need to get over this anger, John!"

"We'll get there soon enough."

Antonio made a fist. "It should've been me. Not Stacey."

"We can't think like that, Antonio. We just dig ourselves a bigger pit."

"I know." Antonio closed his eyes. "But it's hard as heck when you're feeling like this."

"Yes, I feel it, too."

"I just can't get used to the idea that I'll never see her again."

"That's always the hardest part."

"She said it once herself: 'If things weren't meant to work out, then why did God allow me to come back?'"

"You know there's no easy answer."

Antonio nodded. "But God must have *something* in mind. I just need to figure it out."

"He'll help us—in time."

They consoled one another through sheer presence.

"Thank you for coming to see me," said Antonio.

"I'm glad they finally let me."

"I can't wait to get outta here." He pursed his lips. "I need to start doing something useful and productive."

John smiled. "Now you're talking!"

Antonio cast eyes of gratitude upon John. "Thank you for being like a father to me and my brother." He maintained his gaze. "We are who we are in great part because of you. I hope you know how much we love and appreciate you."

"I know," said John.

CHAPTER 52

Satisfied that his visit had done Antonio some good, John rested in a brevity of paternal relief. But, once at home, he had to deal with the issue of Stacey all by himself again. Although being strong for someone else in time of need came with great rewards, it sometimes had a way of draining his ability to manage his own emotions.

When thoughts of Maria drifted in, he thanked God for her.

It seemed that little could replace her feminine touch as of late. Even though he hadn't seen her in a couple of days, they occasionally spoke over the phone. He thought of her all the time now. In fact, he wondered if she might be inappropriately filling Stacey's void.

He had mixed feelings over the matter.

Yet he couldn't deny that speaking with her—even over the phone—made all the difference in the world. Nothing helped him forget his worries better than Maria.

The doorbell brought him out of his daze.

He wasn't in the mood for visitors—at least not until he opened the door and saw Maria holding a dish in her hand.

"How's Antonio?" she said.

"Much better," John welcomed her with a smile. "Please come in."

"I brought you some *flan*. I thought it might help after our last conversation."

He walked her to the kitchen table and brought some plates.

They served themselves quietly.

"Thank you," said John, after his first bite. "It's delicious."

"I'm glad you like it." She tried to probe his introspection. "Something on your mind?"

"It's just hard," said John.

She took his hand. "That's how I felt when my husband died."

"I just don't understand how, of all people, Don had to survive. That's one heck of a sense of humor on God's part, don't you think?"

"Yes, He definitely has a way of things."

He scooped another bite of *flan*. "When I was with Antonio, I tried to maintain a level head as he expressed his anger. But the truth is I felt it just as much as he did."

"It's hard not to."

"What could possibly be on God's mind?"

"It's difficult to say."

"Yes," John reflected. "I suppose the responsibility of knowing all things is too much for anyone to handle."

"At least Stacey's resting in peace now."

"That's for sure," said John.

"I know it's little consolation, but maybe that's why Don's still around?"

John frowned. "Whatta you mean?"

"Maybe God's giving him another chance."

John shrugged at the idea. "I suppose."

"You know God helps us make the most of every situation—even in the midst of our mistakes. He'll get us through *anything*, just hoping that we acknowledge our wrongs and accept His forgiveness. It's only when we reject the path of redemption that we create our own hell."

John reluctantly nodded.

"It brought us closer together."

"Yes," John grinned. "It has done that—which reminds me." He got up and went to get something from the living room couch.

"What is it?"

He came back with a sheet of paper in hand.

"I found this the other day." He handed it to Maria. "It's a poem that Antonio wrote."

She took her time, reading it over several times.

"It's beautiful," she said. "Too bad life isn't always that simple."

"My feelings exactly."

"What's undeniable," Maria asserted, "is that Stacey was a special lady."

"Yes, that she was." John beamed with pride. Such appreciation of someone he loved as a daughter filled him with a joy that refused to go unexpressed. Inspired to his feet, John stretched out an inviting hand, which Maria gladly accepted, and he plucked her to her toes.

When their eyes met, John hesitated. But only for a second.

"You're a special lady yourself," he said.

Maria shied away, at a loss for words.

John gently took her by the chin and restored her gaze.

With her lips quivering, John seized the moment and kissed her for the first time.

She put her palm on his chest.

They forgot about the *flan*—and everything else—until John took her by the hand and led her to the grand piano.

"Are you really gonna play this time?" said Maria.

"Yes."

With fingers on the keys, John gave himself over to Beethoven's "Für Elise."

APPENDIX

ANTONIO QUINTERO'S LAST POEM:

PURE AND SIMPLE

Pure and simple, that's the way I want
Our love and this, which gives it life, to be.
Father, grant them grace from the same font
With which you've granted grace to us. Free
That power behind expressed simplicity,
That childlike power that let's us see
The things we feel we've outgrown, or think
We've outgrown. Remind us how to break
Our pride so that we may rethink
Our priorities. And let us be of the few
That don't take love for granted or fear
Being consumed—shake us, break us, inspire us—
Because when we have faith, we let you do
Your work. When we don't, we interfere.